Becky blew a

And worst of all, become duller than a last period class on the mathematical principles of graphing parabolas and hyperbolas. Without the closeness she'd previously enjoyed with Larry, the new and exciting duties fell flat. What kind of godliness was that? She was supposed to be working for the Lord, not for the pleasure of Larry's company.

Tell my heart that, she moaned inside.

Now, more than ever, she desired to return to the mission field where at least her stimulating adventures weren't clouded by a man's presence. Everything seemed so complicated on the island! And her newfound contentment of waiting upon God for direction was slowly eroding. Larry's nearness and friendship had bolstered her faith and come to mean more to her than she'd realized. Without him, living and working on the island didn't cut it anymore. And she'd only been on the island for what, not even two months? Yet, the distance she felt between them penetrated her very being with a deep and chilly coldness. Like an addiction, she'd come to rely on something or someone she never needed before.

God, what can I do to restore my relationship with Larry? He's a strong and godly man, and I like being around him. I like sharing my ideas and dreams with someone who really listens. Certainly, You sent him to me—I mean, why else would he be around every time I've needed him? If I've done something to offend him, show me how to make it right. I don't want to lose his friendship. Yes, Lord, it does seem out of character for me, but it's true. I—Becky Merrill, the woman who has never needed a man—need Larry.

BETH LOUGHNER is a regular columnist for the Columbus Messenger newspaper and has written for various magazines, as well as three full-length dramas. She began writing in 1990 while enjoying her years as a stay-at-home mom. Beth also finds great excitement in her occupation as a registered nurse. Through her writing, she hopes to inspire others to find the true character of God and to encourage readers to apply these truths to their lives. Her husband and two children have made the beautiful state of Ohio their home. They love traveling to unusual places within the state and beyond its borders.

Books by Beth Loughner

HEARTSONG PRESENTS
HP553—Bay Island

Thunder Bay

Beth Loughner

Heartsong Presents

My husband, Ellis, and children, Jessica and Erica, are my greatest assets. Thanks for being patient while I tapped away at the computer and drifted off to Thunder Bay for long periods of time.

If there were an honor badge for courage and dedication after having a stroke, my father should be awarded such a medal. You have taught me to forge triumphantly on when life gets tough and God allows the pressure cooker to heat up. This book is for you!

A special thanks to my good friend John Pierce. I could never have made it without your endless and talented hours of editing. You stuck by me, knowing I'd never in a million years understand the meaning of a dangling modifier.

For Becky Rickard who is a great encourager and editor who can find those pesky mistakes plaguing all writers. God knew what He was doing when He reunited two old friends last year at Christian camp.

Thanks to Bill Crothers for giving his great expertise on water heaters.

To my good friend Becky Nelson for having the knack for finding errors only seasoned readers see. She's done a great service for those of you bugged by story inconsistencies.

Appreciation goes to Columbus police officer and friend Charlie Sutherland for sharing his knowledge of law enforcement to make this book authentic.

A note from the Author:
I love to hear from my readers! You may correspond with me by writing:

Beth Loughner
Author Relations
PO Box 721
Uhrichsville, OH 44683

ISBN 1-59310-939-3

THUNDER BAY

Our mission is to publish and distribute inspirational products offering exceptional value and biblical encouragement to the masses.

PRINTED IN THE U.S.A.

prologue

Move now! There's no time!

Becky Merrill pulled frantically against the force of the heavy-handed American consulate aide as he gripped her arm tighter.

"Just one more minute!" she pleaded, not daring to take her eyes from those gathered in the room.

The man grunted a negative and proved the point by hustling her through the crudely made doorway into the night. Her luggage bag, clenched tightly in her sweaty free hand, skipped hard across the dirt, the wheels barely touching.

She resisted once more. "I only want to say good-bye—"

"There's real danger, miss." The strong, middle-aged guard paused long enough to fasten his bright blue eyes on her with an accusing light. "I don't particularly want to engage in battle with these commandos, and if you had any sense, you wouldn't either."

"But why the Americans?" she asked in desperation. "We're here to help!"

As soon as the words were out she knew the question to be inane. Hadn't she heard anti-American rumblings at the marketplace just last week? But the people! Her work! How could she leave?

She twisted painfully to see behind as anxious black faces stared back with outstretched arms. Her long black hair pulled across the guard's arm. She hadn't even had time to ponytail the mess in the midnight raid. Tears trickled hot against her cheeks. The heartache of the raw farewell forcing her to leave the Congolese women she'd come to serve threatened to overwhelm her.

They stopped at the army-green jeep, and she took the opportunity to appeal again. "When will it be safe? When can I return?"

She had to wait until her bag was thrown haphazardly into the windowless opening in the back of the jeep before the reply came. The guard turned back to her in a show of tight patience. "You're going to Germany tonight where you and other Americans will be sequestered before flying back to the States. Don't hold your hopes out," he warned. "It could be next month—it could be never!"

The answer seared like a hot poker to her chest. Was it possible she might never return? How could it be? God had placed her in the Congo. Of this she was sure. How could she abandon her post?

All thoughts were rudely interrupted as her five-foot frame was hoisted unceremoniously into the front passenger seat.

"Get in the back," the man commanded before shutting the heavy door. "And keep down."

With resignation Becky crawled to the back, her leg scraping hard against an unseen object. Blood trickled untended down her thigh as she propped herself on both knees to look out the back. The lump in her throat threatened to choke. These people needed her.

"That's it!" yelled another guard as he hopped in the seat she'd just vacated. "Let's go!"

The jeep came to life, and the sound of worn, coarsely grinding gears tore through the night.

The driver heaved an audible and impatient sigh. "Will you get her down?" he ordered the other. "We're not in the clear by any means."

Becky felt a gentle hand tug on her shoulder.

"You won't do those people any good if you get yourself shot," the passenger guard reasoned. "Curl up in the seat and keep your head down."

His gentle tone drew a nod as she complied. He was right.

She must protect herself for the Congolese people, to be ready to return.

But for now the missionary must go home to the States. Just the thought drew another weight onto her already heavy heart. She had no choice. She'd return to the last place she called home—Bay Island!

one

Becky Merrill watched the dangling keys drop into her hand.

"Are you absolutely sure?" Becky asked, her left eyebrow arched in question.

"Absolutely!" Lauren Levitte answered. "I'm finally off on my honeymoon in two days. And I don't need the cabin when I return, do I? You can even use my car for as long as you need it."

Becky relaxed under Lauren's smile. "I'm sorry your honeymoon was delayed by a week, but I'm sure glad you were available when I needed you."

"And I'm happy I was here for you." Lauren gave a genuine smile. "I was disappointed, of course, by the hotel mix-up, but God always knows best and I'm learning to live within His plan instead of mine."

"It's a lesson we're all learning," Becky responded. "He's been so good to work out the details so fast and make Piney Point available at just the right time." She gave a contented sigh. "What a beautiful place to come back to." Both women turned to look at the four-room cabin surrounded by majestic pine trees. The cool spring breeze coming off the lake stirred the heavy branches. Bay Island was once again in blossom after a cold, hard winter. The promise of spring and wedding happiness washed over the inhabitants.

"It seems too good to be true." Becky fingered the warm keys in one hand and straightened the straw hat on her head with the other. "When they rushed me out of the Congo without notice, I literally had no place to go. Bay Island is the only home I've known for two years."

"Bay Island has been a refuge to many," Lauren replied,

casting Becky a mischievous look as she held up her wedding ring as proof.

Becky found herself smiling at the other woman's radiance. The islanders almost gave up hope for Jason Levitte and Lauren, the now happy newlyweds, until Lauren's return last year. Maybe hope would resurrect itself for her, too.

It wasn't just being ousted from the mission field. She was truly and totally alone, ostracized by her family and forgotten by her childhood friends. Suffering from a dysfunctional family might be a newer term, but it was old hat to Becky. Her parents were well-to-do and revered in public. Life changed, however, when the front door closed.

Becky was their one embarrassment. She couldn't muster the grades for the Ivy League school or present the polished grace they demanded. Finding God at a community college only widened the chasm. When she announced her decision to enter missions, they called her everything but a drug-smoking hippie. In their minds she'd entered the cult world. A right-winged Jesus freak, they had said.

Although never spoken aloud, Becky knew she was no longer worthy to be called a Merrill. Rejected, she replied to a job advertisement and traveled far from California to a small island on Lake Erie. Genuinely on her own for the first time, circumstances had cultivated her faith and prepared her for the mission field. There was Michael Petit, though, to consider.

She thought about Michael, still peeved at his behavior at the airport two years ago.

"Come on, Beck," he'd pleaded, planting both hands deep within the pockets of his finely tailored pants. "Why run halfway across the country to work in a sweaty office?"

"It's not a sweaty office," exclaimed Becky indignantly. "Jason Levitte is a reputable architect, and I'm a proficient bookkeeper."

"But it's all unnecessary," he argued, his right hand suddenly grasping hers. "Your father will come to his senses soon. You just have to know how to work him. Religion is good in small doses. It's only that you need to stop being such a fanatic about the whole thing."

Becky felt her mouth drop. Would no one side with her? Michael had been her soul mate at the private high school they'd attended. He was good looking, wealthy, and amusing. He'd made an immediate hit with her parents. Yes, he was made of the right stuff, they told her.

Their college courtship met with her parents' approval, but finding God changed everything. From that time she could feel the added weight of the chains being woven around her. It became evident she must either break free or succumb to their relentless pressure to become what they wanted. She knew God wanted her life totally, not the Merrill leftovers.

"I'll talk with your father," Michael finally said in exasperation. "He's not against religion. Really he's not." Becky watched him roll his tongue thoughtfully around his front teeth and move it away with a smacking sound before he continued. "Maybe you should be a tad bit more delicate in how you come across with your religious beliefs, that's all."

"If that's all there is to it, then why are you so nervous?"

He shook his head. "Not nervous, just concerned."

"Nervous!" she announced. "I've known you long enough to catch every nervous habit you have, and tongue clucking is one of them."

He had the decency to look surprised. "If I do have a nervous habit it's from distress, not nervousness."

"Over my leaving, of course."

"Of course!"

"Then why didn't you stand up for me in front of Father if you were so distressed?" she murmured, steadily meeting his gray eyes. The question seemed fair enough.

Giving her a searching stare, he patted her arm in an almost clumsy gesture. "You know as well as anyone, your father has to be handled with kid gloves. He can be won over, but not with the hit-and-run approach."

"It was hardly hit-and-run, Michael." Becky swallowed the ache in her throat. "What you really mean is that you think I should cater to Father and let him think the matter is dropped—a sort of out-of-sight, out-of-mind approach." She felt a fresh pang of grief. "Then I'm supposed to let him think I'm on a year-long trip to France when I'm actually in the Congo doing missionary work. Isn't that how we've always handled my father, with deception and lies?"

Michael flushed. "Your father necessitates a little creative handling."

"Amen to that!" Becky replied. "But I refuse to make Father happy with lies anymore. He may not be pleased with my choice to be a missionary or my decision to leave California, but at least he knows the truth. When it comes to pleasing God or my father, I have to choose God."

Michael seemed resigned to lose the argument and raised both hands in surrender. "What about us? How are we going to handle living on two different coasts?"

A pent-up sigh escaped her lips. "I don't know."

"Just don't board that plane," he whispered ardently, drawing her into his arms. "I'm afraid of what will become of you."

"Could it be anything worse than what I've endured at home?" she asked softly.

He pulled her back slightly, giving her one of his sweeping looks from head to toe she found disconcerting. "Don't be like that. You'll wrinkle your beautiful skin scowling at me so hard."

Beautiful. Yes, she did have beauty. Her long raven-black hair was the envy of many, and her porcelain skin shimmered like flawless glass. It was hard not to be noticed with the flowing grace that a ten-year commitment to ballet had brought. She often wondered why Michael and her family noticed only the outside appearance and couldn't see the beauty within, the beauty they were crushing with every verbal blow they heaped upon her.

"Michael," Becky said with a sigh, "I'm leaving on the plane. I will work as a lowly bookkeeper for a year until the mission board has my financial support in order. I will be going to the mission field." Her dark eyes considered him again. "Can't you understand my need to do what God wants?"

"No, I don't understand," Michael replied decisively, suddenly willing to take up the battle once again. His arms dropped from her. "How can you know for sure God wants you overseas? Tell me that! Maybe God wants you to stay home and perform your honor-thy-parents duties." His brow smoothed. "I could even pull some strings and get you a job at the church in Turnstile. With five thousand members they'd pay what you're worth. What could be godlier than working in a church—right here in California?"

Becky shook her head in resignation. An unbeliever wouldn't understand. "You've been a good friend to me. I know you don't comprehend, but I'd hoped you'd give me your blessing." Her throat grew dry. "I need your support."

Michael's silence gave his answer. Yet another rejection.

"Flight 157 to Cleveland is now boarding at Gate 12."

Becky shifted to move, but Michael grasped tightly onto her hand.

"Don't go," he begged. "Please."

She knew the plea was hard for him. He'd never pleaded for anything.

"I'm going to be late." She turned away, letting his hand drop heavily to his side. "I'm sorry."

For palpitating moments they measured glances before she quickly walked toward security screening. She recalled her feelings of sheer relief when the plane finally reached for the skies and Bay Island waited with a new life. It seemed like ages ago.

❧

"Hey." Lauren laughed, waving her hand before Becky's eyes. "Are you going to daydream all day or let me help you with the luggage?"

"It seems like only yesterday when I came to the island for the first time," Becky replied with a smile, shaking off her memories. It did little good reliving the past. Michael had kept in touch for only six months. No doubt he'd forgotten her by now. It was time to focus on the future.

Lauren must have sensed her mixed sadness and gave her a light hug. "It's good to have you home."

Becky thanked her and moved to open the trunk of the rental car. The lid slid open noiselessly. One bare bag lay in the compartment.

"That's it?" Lauren asked softly, shifting her eyes back to her.

Becky flushed. "That's all they let me escape with."

Lauren quickly recovered. "No problem. You can share my clothes." Her gaze hurriedly assessed Becky's petite five-foot figure. She tapped her finger across her lips. "Then again maybe we'd better go shopping at Levitte's Landing."

Shopping! Yes, indeed, it was good to be back.

❧

Becky jerked herself up on the bed, her elbows sinking into the comforter. What was that sound? Her skin prickled at the possibilities. The red glow of the nightstand clock read 2:15. It was her second night in the cabin. Jason and Lauren would now be enjoying a gorgeous view of Niagara Falls from their honeymoon suite.

Slowly Becky shoved the smooth covers aside and let her feet sink quietly to the floor. The soft hem of her gown encircled her ankles. She shivered after the warmth of the bed. A small stream of light from outside sprayed a glow across the floor.

Her ears strained to hear the sound of the watery hiss. Several knocking thumps interrupted. Becky moved her feet forward to the hallway where the sounds grew louder. She peeked around the corner into the dark and empty hallway. No one would call her a weak female when it came to nighttime sights and sounds, and she'd hardened even further on the mission field; yet she felt a small sensation of alarm at that very moment.

Shish! Ping, pang, pong.

The cool hardwood floors in the hall creaked slightly under her weight. Her hand skimmed the painted walls to steady her tense body as her head cocked toward the contained clatter. At the kitchen she stopped and felt for the light switch. With one flick the room was bathed in light. Trickling water-like pings continued uninterrupted from beyond the kitchen and into the unlit utility room.

Becky took a steadying deep breath before crossing the cool linoleum floor of the kitchen. Her hand paused momentarily over the knife block before moving on. No, a knife was never good protection when an intruder could easily turn it upon his victim. Past the refrigerator, she stopped again to listen. It was a definite watery sound.

She crept forward. Warm wetness greeted her bare feet before she reached the utility room. Startled, she stepped back. *Water! Plenty of it!* Gathering her senses, she tiptoed forward warily across the wetness to find the light switch of the room. To her relief the water didn't appear to be getting deeper as she paused long enough to feel the walls. *On the right or left?* Nothing but smoothness greeted her hand. As her eyes adjusted slowly to the room's darkness, she saw the white string hanging from the bare bulb.

Click!

Light flooded the room.

Becky drew in a breath at the sight. The forty-gallon water heater hissed and spit water from its base across the floor. The thirsty drain in the center of the small room slurped the clear fluid.

Mildly inclined toward mechanics, Becky could be handy in the house—much to her father's chagrin. Yet she had never dealt with water heaters. She eyed the white monster, letting her gaze drop to the control knob. Bent over to see the markings, she snapped the gray knob to the off position. Still the water hissed across the floor.

Water pipes. There had to be a shutoff for the supply pipe somewhere. Becky gazed up and tilted her eyebrow. She traced the pipes coming and going before finally finding the shutoff lever. Her hand trembled slightly as she reached up toward the lever.

"Four inches short," she snorted aloud in disgust. "I'm always four inches too short."

A glance about the room yielded a yellow ten-gallon bucket, which instantly became the perfect perch when turned upside down. The lever yielded to her touch. Water splattered across her feet as she stepped down. In silence she watched. It took nearly ten minutes before the guzzling water burps slowed to a stop.

Twenty minutes later Becky propped the mop against the wall. Although the floor still gleamed with wetness, it would dry soon enough. In the morning she'd call neighbor Tilly Storm and see about a new water heater. If anyone knew what to do, it would be Tilly. For now, she planned to plop herself, prune-like feet and all, back into bed.

❧

Larry Newkirk rapped on the wooden screen door and waited. His cleanly pressed police uniform felt stiff this morning as he looped one finger inside the collar to give it a stretch. His hand rested over his black gun holster, and the leather creaked with familiarity when he shifted his weight.

"Yes?" A raven-haired beauty suddenly peered at him from the other side of the screen door.

Larry took off his police hat and tucked it under his arm. "Tilly called and said you might need some assistance." He watched her closely, remembering the bookkeeper now. It had been awhile, and she hadn't been an islander long before leaving last year. "I believe she said you had a water heater mishap in the night."

There was a small intake of air before she answered. "She sent the police?"

two

Larry Newkirk had to smile at the woman. The screen cast odd shadows across her face, but he could tell she was beautiful. Tresses of shimmery long black hair encircled her face and the surprised look planted upon it.

"Tilly didn't exactly send the police," Larry chuckled, his head tilting her way. He could feel the sun bouncing off his blond, military-style crew cut. "Besides being a police officer I'm an island handyman of sorts for the church folks." His eyes twinkled. "And when Tilly says jump, I jump."

The woman laughed in return, and a shy smile blossomed. "Please come in." She pushed the door open. "I'm Becky Merrill." She offered her hand.

"Larry Newkirk," he returned, taking her hand. He stepped over the threshold, letting the screen door close behind with a soft bump. "We attended the same church sometime ago, but I don't think we were ever properly introduced."

Once again her smile seemed to light the room. "My schedule was busy during that time. It seemed as if I was visiting one of my supporting churches on the mainland nearly every weekend. I'm sure I know several folks by sight but never met them."

"Tilly said you're a missionary to the Congo."

Her smile faded slightly. "Political unrest made it necessary for me to leave. It's just for a little while." She swiveled her look away from him and nodded her head toward the kitchen. "Coffee?"

"No, thanks." Larry sensed the change in subject. "It'll only take a few minutes to look at the water heater. From Tilly's description it sounds like you'll be needing a new one."

Becky instantly motioned him to the utility room. "It's dry

16

now," she explained, "but the tank was spewing water halfway across the floor in the middle of the night. I'm thankful the room has a drain."

He followed, laying his hat on the dining room table as they passed. "The liner might have split," he offered. "It's a good thing you woke up."

When they reached the utility room, Larry bent on one knee and felt under the tank. Wetness greeted his touch. The gray thermostat cover slid off, and he peeked inside with the penlight he pulled from a black holder attached to his belt. Slowly he pushed himself up. "You'll need a new water heater," he told her matter-of-factly.

A worried expression creased her face. "Lauren's on her honeymoon, and I don't exactly have enough cash at the moment to pay for a new water heater."

The woman's air of vulnerability gave his gut a strange twinge. He was much too sensitive for his own good, he knew. "I think we can find a way to replace the tank now and settle with Lauren later." Withdrawing a small notepad from his shirt pocket he penned several specifics from the tank label. "Harvey's Hardware might have a tank in stock. If not, we'll get one from the mainland by tomorrow."

Becky's expression looked hopeful. "You'll be able to install the new water tank by tomorrow?"

"By tonight if Harvey comes through," he assured her. He had to smile at the look of sheer delight crossing her fair features. She looked ready to burst. Maybe she'd kiss him right on the lips as Mitzi Trammell did when he unclogged her bathroom sink. Being a hero did have its benefits. Although he knew he didn't need any new complications in the world of relationships. His pride still felt the sting of losing Lauren to Jason last year. Well, he didn't really lose Lauren; he'd never had her in the first place. It was all a dream on his part. But still. . .his love life never quite achieved the serious level he'd envisioned.

Larry snapped the notebook shut and stuffed it back into his shirt pocket. "I'll call you by three this afternoon to let you know."

She followed him from the room. "You're an angel sent from heaven."

"Hardly." He laughed pleasantly, taking his police hat from the table. Once again he tucked it under his arm. He stopped and turned when he felt her light touch on his arm.

"It's true," she said with such seriousness. "You can't imagine how God keeps taking care of every difficult detail." Her eyes twinkled. "God's given you special talents. I can feel it. You've probably saved as many people as a handyman as you have by being a police officer."

Larry could feel the heat of embarrassment creep up his neck, but he gave a lopsided grin in response. "I'd hold off judgment until you have hot water again."

"Oh, I have faith," she declared, looking him squarely in the eyes. Her wide eyes opened wider still. "I'm what you call a dreamer. If it can be done, there's always a way. Do you have faith in what God can do through you?"

Silence reigned for a moment, and when he did speak his voice dropped low. "I have a down-to-earth kind of faith," he answered. He didn't want to begin a discussion on the virtues of reality. Let the young lady hang on to her dreams. Most dreams crumble soon enough. This much he knew in his line of business. "I'll give you a call."

She thanked him profusely as he walked out the door and down the wooden steps to his white cruiser. He gave a quick wave of his hand before nudging the car forward.

"Don't get any ideas, Newkirk," he said aloud. "Most women are trouble, and that woman is no exception."

❧

"He's absolutely wonderful," Becky announced to Tilly Storm that afternoon during a visit to her cabin. "He thinks he might even have the new water tank in by tonight."

Tilly gave a hearty laugh, her ample-sized bosom heaving with each chuckle. "So you fell for his charm. Most gals do." She poured more iced tea for Becky. "Larry's one of the finest officers we have on the island. A real gentleman, too."

"I'm not interested in that way," Becky volleyed, holding up both hands in defense. "There's no place in my life for men. I'll be back in the Congo before long."

"Maybe," Tilly said noncommittally. "It never hurts to keep your options open. Why, you can't let yourself mope around Lauren's cabin and do nothing. You never know when a handsome man at your side might come in handy."

Becky glanced at Tilly warily. Tilly was well-known for her matchmaking schemes, and her success rate seemed astounding. "I'll find plenty to keep me busy. There's no room for moping either."

"Glad to hear it," Tilly responded, using even strokes of the knife with her beefy hands to cut the freshly baked bread. Slice after slice fell in perfect order. "I just might have a proposition to keep you busy."

Instantly alert, Becky experienced an odd moment of apprehension. "Am I about to get shanghaied?"

"Absolutely not!" Tilly looked shocked, but Becky didn't miss the devious smile she tried to hide. "Aren't you at all interested in knowing what the proposition might be?"

"Do I have a choice?" she said with a laugh. "What's this plan you've cooked up?"

The motherly woman sat down and served Becky a slice of bread before placing a slice on her own plate. She buttered her piece. She seemed in no hurry, and several seconds passed before she let her gaze fall on Becky. "The church is lookin' to start a Christian camp here on the island. They need a strong leader, a director who can devote some serious time to the project. I think you're that person."

Becky took a sip of her iced tea, listening. "What kind of Christian camp?"

"The camp would be mostly for kids in the summer and a mix of ages for retreats during the fall and spring," Tilly answered. She lifted her slice of bread and pointed toward the window. "Once the lake freezes, though, the camp would be shut down for the season."

How well Becky knew what a harsh winter meant to the island. "So it would be run like most camps where one group of kids stays a week with a speaker and a program? The next week might be the same with a different age group?"

"Yep," Tilly said with a nod. "The camp committee has more details, but you've got the basic gist of things."

"Where do they propose to build the camp?"

"They're lookin' at Thunder Bay."

Becky tilted her head in surprise. "The old Union landmark site?"

"The very one."

Intrigued, Becky asked, "Can you build on a landmark?"

"There're over fifty acres," Tilly explained. "We only need twenty-five to do the job. It's convincing Kelly Enterprises that it can be done without disturbing any delicate historical value."

"Tell me about it."

Tilly seemed pleased with Becky's interest and set the butter-smeared knife across her plate with a clank. "The church has wanted to build a camp for as many years as I can remember. They had their sights set on Frank Ludlow's north shore property, but he sold it to a developer for thousands more than the church could give."

"North Shore's condominiums?"

"Yep," Tilly answered, her lips pursed in disapproval. "Nothin' we could do once city council approved the zonin'. Oh, Ludlow was right sorry after all was said and done. They've ruined the north shore, tramplin' the place with all their litter and whatnot. And they've not held up their end of the bargain with noise curfews." She gave a snort of disgust. "But that's all water over the bridge now. Church folks thought the camp idea was doomed until Jason started lookin' into Thunder Bay. Most of the land is unused. He thinks it can be done."

"He's talked with the owner?" Becky could feel an un-explained excitement grow within. The idea of a Christian camp on the island was perfect. Even if she could only give a few weeks to the project, it would give her purpose.

Tilly nodded her peppery-colored head. "Kelly Enterprises told him it couldn't be done without disturbing the landmark. But Jason's right smart. He's drawin' a plan to show how it can be done. We're hopin' it will do the trick."

Becky took a bite of the warm German bread. "How do you think I can be of help?"

"I knew you'd come on board." Tilly nearly yelped with joy.

"Whoa," Becky chirped. "There are several things to con-sider. First I have to talk with the mission board about my financial support. They have to be in agreement. It's possible the churches might decide to cut my support if I find another so-called job. They might think I'm not planning to return to the Congo."

Surprise overtook Tilly's face. "It's none of your doin'. You'll be doing missionary work of a different sort, that's all."

Becky smiled at how easily Tilly moved problems into neat boxes of logic. Too bad logic didn't rule everywhere. "It may be a form of missionary work, but it's not the work the supporting churches sent me to do. But don't fret." She laid a hand on Tilly's. "I'm interested in finding out more about this camp. If God opens the door, I'll walk through it."

A knowing look came over Tilly. "It's a done deal. Trust me."

❧

The decisive thud of a truck door brought Becky to the wooden screen door. Larry Newkirk was already unstrapping a large cardboard box from the bed of his red pickup. She watched unobserved as he made quick work of the strong twine.

He was handsome in his own right. Maybe twenty-six or

twenty-seven. She guessed him to be at least six feet tall, and his super-short blond hair gleamed against the sun. He looked quite different in straight-legged jeans and a blue T-shirt; yet she sensed he was at home in work clothes as well as a uniform. When he'd phoned earlier, his deep voice could have melted butter. It was easy to see why Tilly was eager to matchmake with the man, but it was ludicrous to think Becky would fit the bill.

What could she offer a man at this point in her life? At best, her plans were short-term. And what man would stick around once he'd met her family? She couldn't ignore the unruly clan forever. One visit with her parents and any sane man would turn tail and run. Only Michael seemed immune. What good was that?

"Hello!"

Becky focused her attention back to Larry who now stood at the bottom of the wooden porch steps. She stepped outside the door and smiled. "I'm certainly glad Harvey came through with a new water heater."

"Your dreaming must have paid off this time around," he said with a returning smile. He motioned directly behind him to the large box strapped to a silver dolly. "It was the last one in stock."

Her tennis shoes thudded softly across the wooden boards as she moved to the edge of the landing. "That's wonderful. I have to tell you again how grateful I am you're doing this."

He seemed to watch her closely. "That's why they call me Handy."

"Who does?" Her eyebrow lifted fractionally.

"All the women, of course," he laughed. "Haven't you ever heard the saying that if women can't find a man handsome, they should at least find him handy?"

Becky smirked. She wasn't about to tell him he was both.

He only laughed at her expression and grabbed the red rubber handles of the dolly. "Get the door—would you, please?"

Becky obeyed, standing back to clear the entrance. The large, awkward box caused the dolly to slap loudly against each step as he pulled the heavy tank backward with even timing. With certainty he rolled the box through the door. Becky followed him to the kitchen where he let the dolly come to rest.

She watched him enter the utility room. He made his way to the corner. The rhythmic squeal of the old valve let her know he'd found the main water shutoff. Suddenly he reappeared.

"Let me grab my tool bag, and I'll be right back."

Becky only nodded and waited patiently. He reappeared a moment later with a small but heavy duffle bag. Without fanfare he dropped the bag on the floor. The zipper gave way with a loud groan as he split the bag open. Several tools were placed in order on the hardwood floor.

Larry stopped rummaging and looked up. "I brought some old towels. Would you mind getting them from the backseat of the truck?"

"Sure," Becky answered, glad to be of help. "Be right back."

Gravel crunched under her feet, and a light wind seemed to sprinkle the air with the scent of pine. Becky took an appreciative breath. In many ways she was glad to experience the familiar smells and sounds of home. The Congo was so different. She had come to appreciate the smallest of things she'd taken for granted before—running water, flush toilets, and even carpeting. One month on the mission field and she'd realized how rich her American home truly was. Excess! After managing on so little, the endless amenities she now experienced seemed like excess.

Becky opened the driver's door to Larry's truck. The four-by-four rested high above the ground causing her to stretch to reach the loose towels on the backseat. The inside of the truck was as she'd imagined. The leather seats were creased from comfortable use, but not worn. A light spicy aroma enveloped the interior. A pair of work boots lay neatly on the mat behind the passenger seat. His police hat sat positioned on the backseat as if placed with care. The gray carpet was clean except for small pebbles of rock and dirt on the driver's mat. Somehow she found the scene calming. This man was methodical and in control.

She gathered the worn towels and held them close. Even these frayed and tatty towels would be a luxury in the Congo. God had blessed her so much throughout her life, and she'd never realized what privileges He'd given her. She'd made a pledge never to forget God's wonderful gifts. Now God had provided a Christian man to fix the water heater. The thought nearly brought tears. Even in her fierce fight for independence, it felt so very good to be on the receiving end of someone else's care. This sudden realization brought both joy and emotional turmoil. How she longed for those in her village to experience such care. A poignant tiredness enveloped her.

"Is something wrong?"

Larry stood less than ten feet from her. She'd been too engrossed in her thoughts to notice his approach. She could feel a warm tide surge into her face.

"I'm sorry," she apologized with a grimace. "You've caught me daydreaming." Once again she hugged the towels close and firmly shut the door of the truck.

He looked unconvinced and inched closer. "From the expression on your face I'd say it's more than daydreaming. Are you missing your friends in the Congo?"

Becky locked her gaze to his. "Am I that obvious?"

"What's wrong with that?" he said with a shrug of understanding. "From what Tilly tells me, in the past week you've not only been forced to leave the people you've come to care a great deal about, but there've been long flights, layovers, and delays." His gaze stayed with her. "Not to mention a lack of sleep last night from an ornery water heater."

She laughed suddenly, caught up in the absurdity of the moment. The man was absolutely right. "You're not only a policeman and handyman, but an observant counselor as well."

"Oh, please," he answered with mocking chagrin. "Don't

start that rumor, or they'll have me working overtime trying to rehabilitate criminals. I can hardly keep up with catching the offenders and scheduling all my handyman jobs."

A smile lit her face. "I promise not to tell."

"Good!" He held out his hand for the towels. "We'd better get back to work if you want hot water sometime today."

Becky gave him the towels. She noticed the roughness of his callused hands and sensed these hands also knew how to be soft. Her lips pursed together in consternation. She had no business with those thoughts. God had sent the man to do a plumbing job, nothing else.

"Ready?" Larry asked, waiting patiently at the foot of the stairs. He directed her toward the steps.

"Ready as I'll ever be," she countered, taking the lead. *But not ready enough!*

three

"That looks mighty fine, it does," said Tilly as she gave the new water heater the once-over. She planted her hand on the doorjamb and leaned back enough to be heard in the kitchen. "What did I tell you about Larry? He does good work."

Becky glanced at Tilly again and pulled two dry plates from the dish drainer. "It's incredible how quickly he disconnected and reconnected everything. The man's amazing."

Tilly smiled at her. "He's a good man, Becky Merrill. They don't make too many like that one."

"He's certainly efficient." Becky opened the cupboard and slid the plates into place on the stack.

"Efficient!" Tilly harrumphed. "Is that all you can say?"

Becky smiled and let the cupboard door close softly. "Handy, too."

Tilly gave a *tsk*. "You'll be findin' out soon enough just how much you'll be needin' his handiness."

"What's that supposed to mean?" Becky narrowed her eyes.

"It means you'll be needin' him to help with the camp project," Tilly explained. "You do realize how much his expertise will be needed?"

Becky wagged her finger in Tilly's direction. "First of all, Larry seems to be a man with enough irons in the fire. He might not have time to help. Second, I haven't given an official okay to directing the project. And third," she went on, "actual building of the camp may be months away. And. . .the committee will have to agree to your assessment that I can do the job. The meeting is tomorrow night, right?"

"That's nothin'." Tilly waved off her protest. "I'm bettin' on you. Not that I'm a bettin' woman, mind you. It's just that you're perfect for the job—and available."

"I've agreed to talk with the committee, but I'm not promising anything," warned Becky. "Besides, there would be several people needed to help, and as I said, Larry may not be interested."

"Oh, I think he'll be interested," said Tilly with a casual nod. "Didn't I tell you Larry's the head trustee of the camp committee?"

A long pause ensued. "No," Becky finally murmured with constrained patience. She shifted her weight to the other foot as she reached across the counter for another dish in the drainer. "I believe you left out that one important detail."

Tilly's lips curved into a smile. "I'm sure I mentioned it earlier. Matter of fact, I called Larry before coming over tonight—you know, just to see if he'd gotten around to your water heater." Her innocent look deserved an award. "I told him you were interested in helping with the camp project. He seemed very excited."

"I'm sure he was," Becky noted with doubt. "What else did he say?"

"Oh, that's all. I told him how much you looked forward to working with him." She held out her hands in a helpful gesture. "Then again I thought you already knew he was chairman."

Becky pulled herself together with an effort and managed a smile. She wondered how she could remain so calm. So far, Tilly had arranged everything from the water heater repair to the camp committee in an effort to push Larry her way. Becky hadn't even been on the island more than a few days. If she didn't know better, she'd suspect Tilly of sabotaging the water tank to set the events in motion.

"I told him to give you a call," Tilly went on. "It would be a good idea for Larry to take you over to Thunder Bay to see the place. That should give you a better feel for the project."

Becky eyed her calmly. "And what did he say to that?"

"He'll call you, of course."

"Of course!" Becky moistened her dry lips. What good would a protest do? Tilly had a one-track mind, and Larry knew Tilly as well as anyone. He probably had a good inkling of the situation.

"I'd better skedaddle. He'll probably call anytime." The woman donned her jacket and rubbed both large hands together with a finishing touch before producing a flashlight from her pocket. She stepped out the door and turned. "Lock the door, you hear."

Before Becky could oblige, the shrill ring of the telephone interrupted.

"Go on now," Tilly instructed. "Lock up quickly and answer the phone." She ambled off, but not before Becky saw a satisfied smile erupt across Tilly's lips.

Becky smirked and firmly shut and locked the door before making her way to the phone.

"Becky?" began the familiar low rumble of a male's voice as soon as she lifted the receiver. "This is Larry Newkirk."

"Good evening," Becky began, feeling more than a little awkward. She took a steadying breath. "Tilly told me you'd be calling,"

"Yes." He cleared his throat. "I think it was more of an order."

Becky flinched. Yes, Tilly had done it now.

"Seems she wants us to discuss the Christian camp," Larry went on. "I must say she had me puzzled about your interest in helping with the camp since you didn't mention it earlier this afternoon."

"It must seem confusing, but Tilly just let me know about your involvement with the camp committee."

He chuckled. "No explanation needed. Where Tilly's concerned, there's more going on than either of us knows."

Relieved, Becky let a laugh escape. "Tilly has several ideas, and the camp is only one of them. She did ask me yesterday about helping with the camp; but she failed to mention you were on the committee, or I would have spoken with you about it today."

"Are you genuinely interested?" he asked with what she could only guess to be concern. "Tilly can be quite persuasive when she wants to be. If you're interested, that's great. We can use the help. But if you're not, you can be honest. My feelings can take it."

Becky gripped the phone tighter. "Actually I am interested and would like to learn more. The camp sounds like a great idea." She paused. "I'm planning to attend the meeting tomorrow."

"Tilly suggested we visit the proposed camp site," he said. "That might be a good idea. It would certainly give you more background into the venture. Would you be interested?"

"I don't see why not."

He seemed pleased. "Great. The meeting starts at seven." A thoughtful silence followed. "There's no sense in both of us driving. How about I pick you up at six to see the property and then we can go to the meeting?"

"All right." She almost finished with her usual banter of "it's a date" but stopped herself. With Tilly's matchmaking schemes she needn't give any encouragement, innocent or not, to fuel the fire. The situation was embarrassing enough.

There was another moment of silence, and Becky felt sure Larry wanted to say more. Evidently he must have thought better of it for he rang off after repeating the time he'd arrive for her the next evening. Becky dropped the phone back into the cradle.

For the next two hours she puttered about the cabin then settled into reading a mystery book Lauren had on the shelf. At last she made her way to the bedroom.

In her room, however, a strange restlessness overtook her, and she finally donned the terrycloth robe left hanging on the hook of the door. The front door unlocked easily, and she pushed open the screen. Her bare feet crossed the cold wood of the deck, and crisp air encircled her ankles. The light wind held a whimsical chill. Leaning against the picnic table, Becky lifted her face upward to drink in the beauty of the night, listening to the stray sounds of an early cricket. In the quietness she could almost hear the muted sounds of a band playing at the Curry Party House near Levitte's Landing.

The moon was rising to fill the cosmos with a silvery light. Looking to the heavens, Becky sent a prayer for the Bantu-speaking people of her village. By now they were rising for the day. She should be rising with them. A long and slow breath gave way to a heavy sigh. *What's Your plan for them, Father? I can't help but feel it was a mistake for me to leave. I'd just begun to gain their confidence. So many of the women were asking the right questions about You. Who will give them the message now?*

Only silence greeted her, and she drew the bathrobe closer.

Please protect them and give the new Christians courage and hope. Send someone to help them.

A sudden groan escaped her lips. Why did it feel as though she were leading two lives? Becky the missionary, and Becky the ex-bookkeeper of Bay Island. Would she take on a third identity as camp director? When she went to the Congo she desperately missed those on the island. Once back in the States she desperately missed her village. Nothing seemed certain anymore. She'd anticipated many things happening on the mission field or at home, but being yanked out of the country in the middle of the night wasn't one of them.

Minutes ticked on as she intermingled musings, questions, and prayers until she had to rub her arms vigorously against the cool of the night. Finally she yielded to the chill and went inside. The warm robe slipped off easily. She slid between the sheets, exhaustion finally having its way. Sleep overtook the night.

*

Larry rested his hand across the steering wheel as the nippy island wind tunneled through the half-opened window.

"Cold?" He looked over at Becky who sat beside him, her hands clasped loosely in her lap.

She turned her attention from the road ahead and flashed him a smile. "Not at all. It's absolutely wonderful. The cool weather is a welcome change."

Still, Larry nudged the electric window up several inches. "I'm guessing the weather in the Congo is warm."

She nodded. "We average in the seventies and eighties year-round. Some days are just plain hot. Warm and rainy is an apt description."

"Seventies and eighties sound good right now. Add plenty of sun, and I'm a warm-weather kind of guy."

"Me, too," she agreed. "I'm not used to Midwest winters."

He cocked his brow. "Where you from? South or West?"

A definite look of reserve crossed her features. "Out West."

Larry watched her shift uncomfortably in the seat and changed the subject. "We'll look at the east side of Thunder Bay first so you can see how much property we're proposing to buy."

The palpable tension eased, and he saw her shoulders relax. "Tilly mentioned the owner might not be willing to sell."

Larry flicked the turn signal. "Kelly Enterprises is what I'd call a mysterious and secretive company." He glanced left before turning. "It's one of those foundations where the owner or owners like to remain anonymous. All of our communications have been by written letters to a post office box, not even e-mail. Since we haven't personally talked with a representative, it's difficult to plead our case. But the landmark is obviously the perfect place for the camp."

Seemingly intrigued, Becky tilted her head. "How long has this Kelly Enterprises owned Thunder Bay?"

"I believe"—he hesitated, thinking—"Kelly purchased Thunder Bay some fifty years ago from another foundation that went belly-up. From what I've heard, the place nearly went to ruins. One thing I do know: Kelly Enterprises had the funds to restore the dilapidated buildings and maintain the landmark since that time."

"That's interesting." She halted then asked, "Do you think Kelly's owned by a family on the island?"

Larry grinned. "There's no one that rich on this island. The foundation owns at least three other Civil War landmarks. Whoever they are, they're a big player."

"Big player?"

Larry gave her a quick look, noting her cautious tone. "Kelly Enterprises carries clout on Bay Island. When the foundation opposed a zoning variance for an alcohol drive-through carryout more than a mile from the landmark, the mayor and trustees promptly nixed the motion." He slowed the truck and pulled into the gravel parking lot. "Needless to say, the island bends over backward for Kelly Enterprises."

She shifted her eyebrow in comment. "From your tone you obviously disapprove. Which bothers you more—the carryout or interference from the foundation?"

"Both." Larry eased the truck to a stop, shifting the gear into park. "I don't like the idea of additional alcohol sales on the island. It makes my job that much more difficult, especially during tourist season. Alcohol generates more disturbances and complaints than any other problem." He gave her the full benefit of his blue eyes. A coldness edged into his voice. "But more than that, I have a greater distaste for talking money."

He heard a slight but sudden intake of breath on her part, but a glance revealed no telltale facial expression on her part. Curiosity caused him to await her response. The moment gave him time to note just how striking the woman looked with her sleek black hair pulled back in a long ponytail. Clad in dress slacks and a long-sleeve blouse, she looked at ease, yet fashionable. Her light complexion probably stayed year round, he reasoned, watching her dark eyes widen at his stare.

She stirred restlessly and shifted her look to the Thunder Bay sign. "So this is the old Civil War site."

"This is it!" He gave her a dry, wry smile. The abrupt change of conversation was apparent. The discussion was over. But why? He'd obviously touched a nerve, not once, but twice during their ride. "Let's take a look around."

Both stepped out and met at the front of the truck.

"This way," he instructed, cupping her elbow with his hand. He steered her toward the pebbled path leading beyond the grove of ornamental cherry trees. Maybe the sooner he gave the tour, the better.

"Absolutely gorgeous," Becky said with awe, touching an early pink bloom of a nearby branch. She turned to Larry. "I've passed this way so many times and never stopped."

Larry smiled in understanding. "I think tourists appreciate Thunder Bay much more than our residents." He pointed ahead. "Just beyond here is a refurbished weaponry building."

The path opened into a large, freshly mowed field. Larry inhaled the earthy smell of the green cuttings. His gait slowed to match hers as she scanned the site.

"What's that building?" With her finger she directed Larry to a rough stone structure with barred windows. "A Union jailhouse?"

"Actually," Larry answered, "that's the treasury. Union money was stored here. The building is nearly indestructible and, from what I understand, one of the few that didn't need major repair."

He turned his attention to three log cabins sitting beyond the treasury. "They dismantled almost every piece of wood in those cabins to rebuild the structure to its previous glory." He cast his look back to her. "I might have been eight or nine years old when the work began."

This seemed to interest her. "You grew up on the island?"

"Born and bred!"

"You're not only knowledgeable, but loyal to the island as well." She smiled.

"Very loyal."

"Loyalty is a wonderful thing." A brief shadow crossed her

face and disappeared. Suddenly she laid her hand on his arm, her fingers cool on his bare flesh. "Is that the property beyond that line of trees?"

Larry nodded and followed Becky as she made her way toward the break in the trees. It was he who had a difficult time keeping up as she steamed forward. Finally they walked into the clearing, and he could hear her light, quick breaths from the lively jaunt. A large, square piece of acreage framed by trees on all sides lay before them. Sunbeams sparkled off the small and irregularly shaped pond to their left.

"This is just one portion of the property we propose to buy," Larry announced, breaking the silence. "Come with me." He led Becky across the field until another opening could be seen.

"Another large field," she exclaimed, completely turning around to view the surroundings. "Look at the shoreline!" The site obviously met her approval.

"It's perfect," he agreed.

"It's also separate from the landmark buildings. I can see why your committee is trying to buy this land." They walked to the shore, and her smile widened. "Eventually you could add sailboats, skiing, and almost any water sport here."

He smiled. "Like I said—perfect."

As they walked back, Becky continually stopped and mentioned potential buildings and possibilities until Larry laughed and held up his hand to stop the onslaught.

"Those are all fine ideas," he admitted, "but not practical."

Becky stopped. "Like what?"

Larry noticed the questioning of her uplifted face. He towered over her, but her enthusiasm seemed to inch her closer up toward him. "The buildings, for example, will need to be built in the first field, not by the lake."

"But why?"

"We need close access to electric, potable water, and to sanitation."

She seemed to digest the information. "Why not run the

electric lines further to the back field?"

"Electric is the least of the obstacles," he pointed out. "There's no village water or sanitary system out this far, and it's impossible to dig a well through the limestone near the lake or to find suitable ground for a leach bed."

"What about closer to the tree line?" She seemed unwilling to give up her idea of lakeside cabins as her gaze panned the collage of tall pines, oaks, and maples.

He flicked an amused glance her way. "The deep limestone doesn't level off sufficiently until the second field."

From her expression he could tell she wasn't satisfied. As they walked back into the first field, she continued offering possibilities. He watched her facial features alternate between consternation and hope. *Right-brained! Definitely right-brained.* He hated popping her dream-bubble again and again, but idea after idea just didn't fit reality. All she seemed to see was a perfect setting. Reality rarely provided such luxuries.

"Your suggestions show plenty of thought," he finally said. "We just need to find a match of ideas with the resources we have."

"I suppose the pond can't be used for swimming," she challenged in response, as they edged near the greenish-colored water.

He sensed her frustration. "Not everything is impossible."

"Isn't it?" She blew a puff of air between her tight lips. "Every idea has an obstacle." She paused. "I don't know. Maybe I'm not cut out for helping with the project. There's a great deal to consider when building a camp. My skill level might not be of help."

Larry drew his eyebrows together. "As I said before, you have plenty of good ideas. But reality is hard. Dreams are great as long as they stay grounded with realism."

She began walking toward the pebbled path but suddenly stopped and turned to him. "Are you a half-empty or half-full kind of guy?"

"What?" He threw her a puzzled look.
"Oh, never mind. It was a nonsensical question."
"If you say so."
"I do."

four

Becky snapped her seat belt in with a decisive click. She heard Larry do the same. The trip was informative, but far from productive. She pursed her lips in thought. Larry knew the technical aspects, the bricks and mortar, so to speak, of building a camp. But it was possible, she had to admit, he might lack the ability to go beyond the obvious obstacles.

With such a beautiful lakeside view it seemed criminal not to look at every possible angle to build the cabins near that very spot. With some ingenuity they might overcome those pesky details of potable water and leach beds. It wasn't as if Larry didn't have the skill, she reasoned. He certainly had his facts straight. He just needed to think outside the box. Dream a little!

Becky stole a glance his way. His handsome face had a no-nonsense look, the facts-and-figures presence that made him seem so strong and fiercely dependable. Nurturing, too! Most women would jump at the chance to work with the man. He even had a sense of humor. And who could forget that memorable night a year ago when he captured a burglar outside Lauren's cabin? The entire island talked about nothing else for months, so Lauren had written her. To hear of the residents' endless chatter, he was an island hero. She turned her gaze back toward the window. It wouldn't do to daydream about the guy. An unpredictable future meant an unpredictable life and no room for relationships. Besides, he was a bit of a pessimist.

The red brick church came into view, and the truck drew smoothly to a halt. He seemed as relieved as she was for the drive to end. The same rather strained silence persisted as they entered the side door and walked the long hall to the small multipurpose meeting room. Ten chairs surrounded one lone table. Larry directed her to sit next to him at the far end.

A few members greeted Becky. Church librarian Mrs. Phillips and her close friend Lottie BonDurant brought refreshments and begged Becky to try their best brownie concoction. Others filed in, but none brought anxiety like church elder Mr. Edwards. Now here was a gentleman no one, least of all Becky, wanted to cross. Certainly he did more than his share of work for the church, but he was more than cantankerous as well. Notoriously! And he never missed a business meeting. How well she remembered why a twenty-minute meeting could stretch into eternity. The last she'd heard, he was working at the Dairy Barn running the cash register and cleaning tables. Money was an issue, local gossip whispered. Most felt little pity. It took only one personal introduction to his barbed tongue to lose the sympathy.

She smiled when Lottie rolled her eyes as Mr. Edwards seated himself opposite to Becky. She'd have to keep an open mind. He was, after all, a child of God.

The room hushed as Larry commanded their attention and opened with prayer.

"We have quite a few updates," he began after prayer, still standing at the head of the table. "I'd like to bring the committee up to speed on current finances." Larry circulated copies of a financial statement. "We also have Becky Merrill with us tonight. She's considering the job of camp director for the interim. Most of you heard on Sunday that Becky will be with us until it's safe for her to return to the mission field."

Becky felt all eyes on her, and she gave an acknowledging nod. Lottie patted her hand as Larry introduced each member. He quickly moved on.

"We are still awaiting a response from Kelly Enterprises to our proposal," Larry announced. "As you can see from the financial statement, we can negotiate a substantial offer for the property—"

Immediately a low grumble erupted from the white-haired Mr. Edwards. "Don't know why we have to go about disturbing a historical landmark. I've said it before—it's sacrilegious!" A following *harrumph* punctuated his disapproval.

Both Mrs. Phillips and Lottie raised their eyes to the ceiling in unison.

Larry took in a slow, deep breath, and Becky knew he was keeping his anger in check. "We've already been through this, Mr. Edwards. As we discussed before, the Civil War landmark and the camp can coexist together. I was planning to share additional information proving the fact later in the meeting, but since the subject has been brought up I'll discuss it now." He shuffled through his folder, finally producing a typed letter. "The Bay Island Department of Commerce has provided a recommendation for us to use during negotiations with Kelly Enterprises. A recent tourism study indicates a project such as our family-friendly camp on the unused portions of Thunder Bay's acreage could easily generate twenty-five percent or more tourism for the island."

"I'd like to see that letter," Mr. Edwards demanded, holding out his hand.

Larry offered the paper and continued talking as Mr. Edwards brought the print within two inches of his thick glasses. "Allowing the camp to build on the property also predicts a sizable increase in visitors to the landmark itself—a definite benefit for the foundation. Kelly Enterprises has devoted thousands, if not millions, to preserving history and educating the public about the past. What better way to achieve their goal."

"Interesting," said Mr. Edwards, sliding the paper across the table at Larry. His voice conveyed a wealth of intonation in his simple response, and Becky glanced cautiously back at Larry. It would take more than a spoonful of grace for Larry to deal with the inferred challenge.

"It's more than interesting," Larry assured him in measured

tones. He let his eyes roam the room of members. "No one is more conscious of the importance of the landmark than I am. It's part of our history, the history of Bay Island and our people. That's what makes it perfect. Like other residents I watched Thunder Bay be restored with such historical accuracy that, as a child, I felt as if I were being transported back in time. We would never let the camp infringe on that heritage but protect and encourage others to see God's hand in its preservation. Its resources are too valuable to be lost."

Becky's heart warmed at his short, impassioned speech. It was from the heart, she knew. Maybe a dreamer did lie dormant beneath his pessimistic exterior.

Mr. Edwards seemed moved as well. "It is something to think about, young man."

"With the commerce department endorsing our idea," Larry added, "it has given solid evidence to back our decision. I feel this is an answer from God and an indication we are following the path God would have us to take. We need to give Kelly Enterprises the chance to decide. If God wants the camp at Thunder Bay, God will provide it."

Lottie slapped her palm decisively on the table causing Becky to jump. "I'm with Larry. This is the best news we've had in a long time. I say we show this letter to Kelly Enterprises and see what God has in store for us."

Becky watched the other members bob their heads in agreement. Her gaze finally rested on Mr. Edwards. His lips whitened slightly from the taut expression.

"I suppose it wouldn't hurt," Mr. Edwards grudgingly agreed.

"All right," Larry acknowledged with a deep intake of air. "I'll contact Kelly Enterprises immediately with the letter. We'll accept God's answer—" He looked pointedly at the white-haired elder. "We'll accept the answer—whether yes or no."

A murmur of approval spread throughout the room, followed by an elongated pause. When Mr. Edwards remained silent, Larry continued.

"The next item on the agenda deals with the position of camp director." He gave Becky a supportive smile. "The job of camp director is outlined on this sheet." Larry raised the duplicates in the air. "Please take a copy and review the description." He divided the papers and handed a set to Becky and another to Mr. Edwards. The papers shuffled noisily down both sides of the table. "The job is currently limited to idea building and coordination of various aspects of design, planning, volunteer staffing, and general duties. At this point the job is on a volunteer basis, although Becky believes the missionary agency will continue her financial support at least through the summer." Larry paused. "There's also the possibility she might be called back to the Congo or financial support might be terminated. We'll cross that bridge when and if we need to. For now, she is willing to give of her time to help with the project." He smiled at Becky. "Becky, you might want to say a few words."

Becky suddenly felt her palms grow sweaty, and she clutched them together nervously under the table. She wouldn't dare look at Mr. Edwards. "If you believe I can be of help, I'd be glad to do what I can as camp director." A slight smile lit upon her lips. "It's different from anything I've done before, but I hope my experiences in accounting and my head for facts and figures will be useful."

Larry nodded in support, but his laid-back features quickly dimmed when Mr. Edwards stood to his feet.

"Does Jason Levitte know about this?" The old man looked sternly at Larry through thick eyeglasses. "He should be here."

"Here we go again," whispered Lottie loud enough for several to hear.

Becky stirred uneasily and risked a glance at the elderly man. This meeting was becoming an emotional landmine. Obstinate would be too kind a word for Mr. Edwards. He wasn't known to mince his words lightly or with congeniality, but this was ridiculous.

"Jason and Lauren are on their honeymoon," Larry responded. He paused; not a muscle of his face moved. "I haven't spoken to him for this reason, but he's worked extensively with Ms. Merrill in the past and will no doubt welcome her help without reservation."

Mr. Edwards squinted his enlarged blue eyes. "But we've never discussed having a woman for camp director. With construction and technical details, certainly it's a man's job."

Becky heard several members gasp in astonishment and displeasure. Her heart turned over. No wonder Larry leaned toward being pessimistic over camp details if every itty-bitty item had to be squeezed through Mr. Edwards's tight grasp. Dragging a ball and chain would be easier. How should she respond to someone so unreasonable? God would have to help her. She was usually even-tempered, and anger didn't come easily; but any minute now she might explode. Desperately she tried to assemble her thoughts into some sort of godly, coherent order.

But Larry was already trying to soothe the tense air. "I'm sure, Mr. Edwards, you didn't mean that to come across as it did—"

"I most certainly did." The old man gave a punctuated sniff. His gravelly voice continued. "This is a man's job! And I say—"

Larry cut him off at the pass. "We've swam these waters before, and unless a new life jacket has been purchased I respectfully suggest this line of discussion be dropped." He was using his police-authority voice Becky knew would stop most in their tracks.

Good for you. She silently applauded him. Unfortunately Mr. Edwards ignored the warning and didn't seem inclined to forgo the issue just yet.

"Ms. Merrill has admitted she doesn't have any experience being a camp director," he stated. "Just because she comes free of charge doesn't make it right."

This brought Mrs. Phillips and Lottie bounding to their feet like identical twins with agility beyond their age. Larry's muscular jaw began to work, and he seemed ready to release whatever handle he had on his anger; but Becky was quicker than either.

"Please, Mr. Edwards," she pleaded, praying for calmness and control. "I'm not trying to take over the project." She motioned to the standing ladies and the old man. "Please sit down." Becky glanced at Larry and spoke carefully past a sudden constriction in her throat. "You're right. I don't have experience designing structures, building frames, or putting up drywall, but if someone would show me how, I'd help. Not because I'm a woman, but because I'm God's servant." She had to smile—God made her words sound so good and spiritually sound. "Give me a chance to see if my skills can be used. If not, I'll eagerly hand over the responsibilities to someone better."

"Well. . ." Mr. Edwards seemed to think over the proposal.

Feeling much more confident Becky continued soothingly, "If it helps, just think of me as Larry's right-hand woman."

The minute the words escaped, her eyes widened in horror. What had she just said? It had come out wrong—so wrong. Even though Larry was smiling, she could see the familiar red climbing up his neck. Mr. Edwards squinted as if it were too much to comprehend, and the two ladies giggled. How she wished she could melt and slink under the table.

Stunned silence continued until Lottie spoke. "We all know what you meant, dear. Now, if Tilly were here, well, you might not be off the hook so easily."

Becky heard Larry laugh softly at that, and after a moment's hesitation she laughed as well. "Before digging myself any deeper, I'll rest my case."

"Wise idea," Larry said low enough to be heard only by her.

The tension-filled room suddenly brightened, and everyone, including Mr. Edwards, grinned.

"May I have a motion to accept Becky Merrill as interim camp director?" Larry asked, obviously taking advantage of the lighter moment.

Unanimously accepted, Becky swallowed her trepidation. Reprieved! She'd defended her position for a job she wasn't even sure she wanted—and won—and managed to embarrass herself in one fell swoop. Only God could orchestrate such an event.

five

Becky coaxed her sleek black hair into a smooth knot at the nape of her neck. Hurriedly she slid her arms into the light blue jacket. Larry had called fifteen minutes earlier with exciting news about Thunder Bay and asked to meet at Jason's home within the hour. He was unusually evasive, but she could tell he was ecstatic. It could only mean Kelly Enterprises agreed to sell.

The honeymooners had returned two days ago, and Becky smiled at the thought of their happiness. She would be glad to see them. It certainly seemed more than two weeks since they'd left. Plucking the keys from the counter, she snugged the door shut and locked the dead bolt. The small car came to life, and Becky descended the short incline toward the shoreline. So much had happened in a week.

The thought brought a groan. Things had gone smoothly until the mail arrived yesterday. If only Larry hadn't been with her at the time. Now she almost dreaded seeing him, to face his questioning glances again.

Larry had visited the day before to show her the results of a preliminary land survey for Thunder Bay. There might be hope for one or two cabins by the shore after all, he'd said.

"The survey is unofficial," Larry warned, sitting down on the top step of the deck outside her cabin. "A friend of mine gave a cursory examination of both parcels as a favor. It might be more expensive, but doable. We'll have to wait on Jason to see what he thinks."

Pleased, Becky beamed and sat beside him. "Thank you for believing enough to at least give the idea a chance. That means a lot to me." She felt a tinge of warmth come into her cheeks. "I'm really getting excited about the camp. The initial drawings from Jason you gave me the other day are fantastic. And God's going to come through with the land; I can feel it." She began to peruse the land survey documents. "Have you heard anything at all?"

"We should have an answer any day."

She flipped a page and held it in front of her. "How interesting."

Larry leaned closer to see. "Aerial map of the site."

"Your friend did these?"

"It pays to have friends in high places."

Becky laughed at his teasing and pointed to the map. "Whose land abuts the Thunder Bay shoreline property to the west? That's the only house close by."

"That would be Mayor Thompson's place," he answered, continuing to look over her shoulder. He pointed to the faint outline of a boat dock on the property. "Mayor Thompson used to let us dock our family's boat during the summer at his place. He's a good guy, almost like a second father."

Astonished, Becky asked, "He's been mayor since you were a kid?"

"Yep." There was a laugh at her expression. "Twenty-seven is not *that* old."

She lightly slapped his arm. "That's not what I meant, and you know it. It's just unusual for people to stay in a public office that long. People don't usually hang around in one place for any length of time."

Larry seemed to ponder her statement. "So you've said before."

"What?"

"Oh, I don't know," he answered with care. "You've mentioned on occasion how hard it is to find people devoted to their roots." He paused a little before continuing. "Did your family move around a great deal when you were younger?"

The seemingly innocent question put Becky on full alert.

How could she tell him how her family progressed steadily from lower class to high class, buying bigger and better with every move? How her father moved heaven and earth to provide what he deemed to be deserved? It didn't matter who stood in his way; they were merely stepping-stones providing a way to the prize. It was always move on and move up. Perhaps her parents had moved on and up again during her time in the Congo. There had been no contact since she'd left California.

"Does talking about your family make you nervous?" His gentle voice, however tender, increased her anxiety to new heights.

"I don't have much family to speak of," she finally responded, rubbing her hands together in apprehension. What would he say when he discovered she was disowned? Her head swam with the knowledge. She wasn't to blame, right? But her heart wondered what kind of disappointment she must be to cause a mother and father, dysfunctional or not, to stoop to such measures.

"Do you want to talk about it?"

She risked an upward glance. "Maybe someday, but not today."

"Sure?"

"There's not much to tell." She turned her gaze to the tall pines, knowing her words weren't true. "It can wait." Her heart ached to tell someone—someone like Larry. How easy it would be to lean close and tell him how her heart burned in humiliation. But she wouldn't. She was already dangerously close to enjoying Larry's company more than planned. It just wouldn't do. She was confused and vulnerable—hardly a worthy state of mind when making decisions about a relationship, especially one she wasn't free to give. His caring demeanor, however, touched her heart as nothing before, and she feared this might be her undoing. And he was available— too available, too close.

"I'll be here when you care to talk." His hooded look stayed with her. "I'm a homebody and not going anywhere."

She raised her head again and saw his face was quiet and grave, his blue eyes unfathomable. "I believe you. You're so much a part of this island."

"Born and bred!"

"So you've said before." She repeated his previous line.

"That's why this camp project is so important," he went on, shifting the subject matter back to safer ground, much to Becky's relief. "The church has tossed around the idea of a camp for so many years; it seemed more like pie in the sky than reality. It's hard to believe the time has come, and it's actually approaching fruition. We're so close."

Becky instinctively laid her hand on his arm. "You've worked so hard on this project. God will bless you for it."

"He already has." He laid his other hand over hers.

She glanced up and locked her gaze with his bright blue eyes. He meant her! It was written clearly across his face. He liked her, was interested in knowing her better. It was all there. The revelation warmed her very core—yet trepidation still lay heavy on her heart. How effortless it would be to fall for a man such as Larry. In the few days she'd known him, he'd been attentive to her needs and those of others. What else could she say; he was a man of character, exactly what she would want— if she were looking.

The sound of an approaching mail truck broke the silence and drew their attention to the road. The flag went up on the mailbox at the end of the drive.

"I've got mail," she whispered with obvious distraction, unwilling to break the moment. Then the thought hit her, and she sat straight up. "I've got mail!"

"That would be an echo."

Feeling suddenly lighter, she laughed. "You don't understand. I've been awaiting word from my people in the Congo. Maybe a letter has finally come."

"Want me to fetch the mail for you?" he asked lazily.

She shook her head. "Let's go together."

As one, they descended the steps and walked the long pine-covered drive. The emotional tension had since evaporated, and Larry seemed back to his usual self. Laughing, he feigned an attempt to reach the mailbox before she did. Becky sped past him.

"Keep your scratchers off," she teased, opening the box. "This is only my second time to get mail since arriving on the island. I can't afford to miss even one letter." One letter did lie in the box, and she snatched it, laughing as he tried to see it. "Back off, Buster!"

He playfully retreated, both hands up in surrender. She held the letter mischievously within sight but out of his reach. Her good humor, though, suddenly took a dive when she saw the Sacramento postmark.

"Something wrong?" Larry asked, his voice immediately filled with concern.

Becky was silent. Unbidden memories returned to her mind. Michael! A letter from Michael. How did he know she was on Bay Island? She hadn't even told her family. Her past rushed upon her, and a shiver of anxiety coursed up her spine. Complications! Always complications. And Michael Petit was one big complication.

&

Larry held open the front door and greeted Becky and immediately helped her slip out of her light blue coat. "Jason and Lauren are in the sunroom," he announced, pointing to the back room.

She nodded and thanked him as she pulled several wisps of stray hair away from her rosy cheeks. "I rushed over as soon as I could." Her features became animated. "It's Thunder Bay, isn't it? We have the property!"

He laughed. "Sorry, but you'll have to wait. Jason wants to break the news." Steering her across the formal room, he felt his leather boots sink into the deep pile of the honey gold carpet. "Everything okay?" he asked in a low voice.

A shadow crossed her face, but she smiled. "Just fine."

Liar! From her expression it was evident all was not well, and it had to do with the letter she'd received yesterday. It was postmarked from Sacramento; at least he'd seen that much before she hurriedly stuffed it into her pants pocket. Whoever sent the mail caused the woman to clam up faster than a criminal claiming the fifth.

"Becky!" Lauren immediately accosted Becky as they entered the room.

Larry watched for several moments as the two hugged and exchanged updates. Some of the strain seemed to leave Becky's face. He'd give his eye teeth to find out about that letter. A deep and frustrated breath filled his lungs. That was his trouble. Something drove him to be the white knight, rescuing lost souls and feebly attempting to fix the world's problems. And Becky was his worst case. Since laying eyes on her anxious face the day he'd arrived to fix the water heater, he'd thought of nothing else. He wanted to help, to know her better, but she purposely kept him at arm's length.

"Take a seat."

Larry turned to look at Jason and smiled. Jason shrugged his shoulders and with a knowing grin pointed to the table and tall wooden stools set next to the window. "They might be awhile."

Larry perched himself on a stool and hooked the heel of his boot on the cross bar beneath. "Don't mind if I do."

"Heard you took care of a water heater problem at the cabin while we were gone." A note of amusement filled Jason's voice.

"A Tilly referral."

Jason burst into laughter. "Ouch! What did that cost you, and I don't mean the labor? Are you engaged yet?"

"I was on duty that morning, and poor Becky thought Tilly had sent the police over to help." Larry chuckled, trying to keep his voice out of range of the ladies. "And you know Tilly. I'm almost certain the woman knows everything that goes on. She probably had a hand in putting the water heater out of action."

"Did it work?"

"Well, let's see," Larry began. "We're working together a couple of times a week on the camp project and on the phone even more often. I'd say Tilly's in her glory."

Jason seemed to find the whole ordeal innately funny. "Oh, before I forget," he said, reaching into his pocket and handing over a check. "Here's the payment to take care of the water heater expenses. Will that cover it?"

"Whoa! Too much." Larry passed the check back. "The tank was only—"

Jason pushed the check toward him. "Doesn't matter. I'm taking into account your labor and short-notice availability." When Larry didn't budge, Jason stubbornly shook his head. "I'm not taking it back."

Reluctantly Larry folded the check and tucked it into his wallet. When he slid the wallet into the pocket of his jeans and looked up, Becky was at his side, obviously seeing the check exchange.

"I hope it was okay about the water heater, Jason." Becky looked anxiously from Jason to Larry. "I didn't know what else to do. And Larry did such a good job—"

Jason patted her arm. "You did exactly what we would have wanted."

"Are you sure? I can pay you back."

"It's fine, Becky," Lauren reassured her. "Actually I'm the one who feels bad about this happening to you. It must have scared you to death in the middle of the night. I should have changed the tank last year. It was older than Methuselah."

Larry could still see Becky's apprehension, her vulnerability surfacing again. Obviously she wanted to pay for the water heater but was embarrassed not to have the resources to do so. It was preposterous, really. As a guest at Piney Point, she must know maintenance items wouldn't be her responsibility. Hotel guests didn't change burned-out light bulbs or loose towel bars, did they? He wouldn't count the time he fixed the broken showerhead on his last trip to Dallas for a conference. Chalk that up to compulsive behavior on his part—hardly normal for the general public. Yet, from the look on her face, she was equating her situation with a handout.

This gave Larry some thought. Maybe she came from a family who worried over money, a tight income. Could this be the reason for her hesitancy in talking about her family? She did seem disturbed when he discussed the issue of talking money. Still it didn't make sense. Even in the short time she'd known him, certainly she knew he wouldn't look down on one's financial status. Money wasn't everything!

Another thought hit him. Maybe she came from money! He looked at Becky again and quickly dismissed the idea. He'd seen his fair share of rich folks during tourist season, and Becky didn't fit the bill. She'd never fit in. No, he'd have to give another path of thought more time to form. Right now, though, it seemed as if their small group was ready to assemble.

"Shall we talk about Kelly Enterprises?" Jason asked, motioning for all to sit around the table. "God has pulled off the most remarkable feat, over and beyond what we even prayed."

"I knew it," Becky exclaimed excitedly, already seeming to set aside her previous problems. "Kelly's going to sell."

"Better than that!" Jason gave Becky a neatly folded letter. "Kelly Enterprises is donating the land."

Becky unfolded the sheet and read the letter carefully, her face radiating joy at the news. "This is unbelievable! How did we go from the foundation showing no interest to a land donation?"

"It's a God-thing," Larry offered. "I think this fits under the oh-ye-of-so-little-faith category. And you realize what this means—"

Clearly the others knew, but puzzlement crossed Becky's face. "What?"

"It means," Larry continued, "the monies earmarked for the

purchase of the land can be used for building. Jason has the first-phase designs nearly completed, and once an official land survey is conducted and permits obtained, we can break ground."

"How soon?" Becky seemed breathless by the news.

"A month, maybe two."

Becky clapped her hands together. "This is fantastic!"

"And a reason to celebrate," Lauren chimed in. "That's why we wanted you to come over. Jason's treating us to dinner at the Landing tonight. Please tell me you're both free." She looked at Larry and Becky. "Jason will bring the designs, and we can set the plans into motion."

Larry gave a shrug. "Don't see why not."

"Absolutely!" There was no hesitation on Becky's part.

Pleased, Lauren gave Jason a kiss on the cheek. "I'm starved. Can we go now?"

"I'll get the car," Jason announced, already standing.

Outside the sun pleasantly warmed the cool air. With an even stride Larry walked behind Becky, his boots sounding heavy against the concrete walk. He opened the back door of the black sedan and helped Becky, her coat draped over her arm, climb into the backseat. He slid in next to her. She turned and gave him a smile.

He leaned toward her. "Did you bring the aerial maps? Jason will want to see them."

"Yes," she answered, digging into her purse. "I put them in my purse right away after you called so I wouldn't forget." The small packet slid out easily, and she handed it to him. Another object landed in the seat between them.

Larry recognized the object as the letter she'd received the day before. She rushed to grab the letter from the seat and jam it into the middle compartment of her purse. Then with great effort she tried to close the zipper, but her clumsy attempt only wedged the zipper into the material.

"Let me." Larry reached over and worked the zipper until it gave way and closed.

"Thank you." She managed a smile, an impish one at that. "Rescued again."

"No problem."

Oblivious to the charged atmosphere, Jason began to engage them in a discussion about Thunder Bay. Becky participated with vigor. Larry, however, didn't miss the slight change in her demeanor. Something powerful lay within the envelope now tucked safely inside her purse. But for now he could only wonder at its contents.

*

Becky kept a tight grip on her purse, her face growing warm under Larry's scrutiny. It took all of her courage to meet the gaze that regarded her so intently. Of course the letter had to fall out of her purse. What rotten luck. It wasn't as if she could forget the note, even if she'd tried. Michael's words were memorized, emblazoned within her mind.

> *My dearest Rebecca,*
>
> *News has reached home about your hasty and dangerous departure from Africa. I contacted the missionary board who gave me your forwarding address, but of course I had hoped you might call. The gentleman wouldn't give additional information on your welfare. Are you all right? Your parents are sick with worry. Please call me when you receive this letter. We can work out our differences enough to be friends, can't we?*
>
> *Lovingly,*
> *Michael*

Becky would have to make the call soon; that much she knew. Michael wouldn't go away without an answer. The letter was already a week old, and Michael was not a man known for his patience. She'd make the call, but right now she wanted to concentrate on Thunder Bay. God had exciting things in store for the project.

six

It took a long time for the island sun to rise up over the peak of the trees in the morning, and yet to Becky it seemed as if it was down again before one knew it, slipping and sliding behind the cabin. She was thankful daylight hours were steadily increasing with the warmer temperatures. She stretched languidly in the comfortable bed, aware the sun was pouring in through a gap in the curtains. It most certainly was late in the morning. Her brain refused to shut down during the night, and now she was feeling the tiring effects.

It came as no surprise when after lunch she plopped down on the porch lounger ready for an afternoon siesta. The first unseasonably warm day since her arrival lay in wait, and she plumped the cushion with her hands until the firmness felt just right, contouring perfectly to her exhausted body. In the distance the faint blare of the ferry horn blended with hundreds of seagulls squealing their call, no doubt looking for the bounty of fish brought near the surface from the churning propulsion of the boat. The vision brought a smile to her lips. Home never sounded so good. She took a satisfied breath and reveled in the sun's warmth against her skin as it released the fragrance of tropical coconut from the sunscreen she wore. Slowly she felt the weight of her eyelids grow heavy.

Becky knew she must have slept, for she awakened with a sixth sense telling her she wasn't alone. Slowly her dark eyes opened, and her head turned almost of its own accord.

"Don't look so unbelieving," said the man beside her. "It's really me." He laughed at her wide-eyed look. "I'm not the bogeyman."

Becky felt her face pale. "Michael!"

"Yes?"

She sat up. "What are you doing here?"

"At the moment," he said, "watching you sleep." His full lips twitched. "Is life so easy on the island you can laze away the day sleeping on a chaise lounge?"

Becky could only stare at him. He was sitting on the picnic table bench within a foot of her, watching closely with his intense gray eyes, his dark curly hair exactly as she remembered. His expensive, dark blue sports jacket opened wider as he leaned back with his elbows on the table.

"You didn't answer my letter, Rebecca," he chided.

Becky's lips parted silently. If she could have found something to say, though, Michael didn't wait to hear what it was.

"Don't look so chagrined. It's your own fault I'm here, having to travel across the country to find out if you're in one piece. Your father is in a true snit."

Becky found her voice. "But I was going to call tonight."

"Really?"

"I was!" she said almost resentfully. "I'm very busy working on a project."

"So I see!" His eyebrows lifted then suddenly smoothed. "Let's not argue. I've crossed enough miles in one day to drain a person. Then there was the awful ride in a rental car from Cleveland— only to find out I couldn't bring the car across on the ferry. Who knew the island restricted motor traffic to those with lodging reservations? And now"—he motioned to the white golf cart on the gravel drive—"I'm reduced to renting an archaic Flintstone mobile. I should think after all that I deserve a better welcome."

"I'm sorry," she managed, desperately collecting herself with effort. "You've shocked me, that's all."

He laughed, a deep, hearty laugh, his teeth a brilliant contrast of whiteness against his dark tan. "I can only hope it's a good shock." He looked at his gold wristwatch. "A major portion of the day is already wasted, and we have a great deal to talk about. Now be a gracious hostess—get up and fetch us something cold to drink. I'm dying of thirst."

"Of course." Obediently she swung her legs over the side of the chaise.

Michael had changed little in appearance or behavior. His handsome features were somehow deeper, sharper. . .more mature. Yet his smoky gray eyes still held their usual mesmerizing quality, which sparked to life just before the flash reached his lips. Becky became keenly aware of his masculine cologne assailing her nose as he leaned across the space between them.

"Come on," he said, offering his hand. "I'll help you up."

Flustered, she waved him off. "I'm all right." She stood to her feet. "You might as well come inside." Leading the way, she held the door until he took its weight and advanced to the kitchen. She opened the refrigerator. "Juice, cola. . ."

"I could really use a wine cooler." Michael had pushed his hands into his tailor-made pants pockets, regarding her in an enigmatic fashion.

"Sorry!"

"Beer?"

Becky frowned at him. He was testing her, knowing good and well she wouldn't have alcohol. "Sorry."

"Oh, very well, I'll have a cola."

She pulled two cold soda cans from the shelf and rinsed the tops in the sink. "Glass and ice?" Without awaiting his nod she opened the cabinet door and produced a tall glass. Michael never, ever drank from a can. The snap of the lid followed by the clinking of ice rang loudly in the silence; even the fizz of soda seemed to reverberate in the room. "Here you go."

Michael accepted the glass, leaned against the kitchen wall and took a long drink, never letting his gaze waver from her direction. "You've changed."

"I suppose we both have." Becky took a sip from her can, not missing his slight wince as she did so. "Two years is a long time apart."

"Too long!"

She returned his stare in silence. "You said Father's upset," she managed to say, trying to break the spell. "How are Mother and Father?"

"Heartsick." He motioned her to the living room. "Shall we sit?" When Becky followed and sank into the sofa beside him, he continued. "You really have been negligent in contacting them. You must have known they would hear about the evacuation and be worried."

Heat flooded her face. "That's hardly fair, Michael. When I left two years ago Father made it clear there was no turning back. He severed relations with me, and. . .it hurt deeply. They expressed their wishes to hear from me only if I gave up this"— she drew quote marks with her curved fingers—"absolutely horrid cultlike fixation."

"I think they've softened," he offered.

She shook her head. "That doesn't seem likely. Neither of them has attempted to contact me here or abroad."

"Some developments recently have changed that."

Startled, she looked at him, aware of a sudden tremble. "Something has happened? They aren't well?"

Michael's face became grim. "Your mother suffered a slight stroke nearly three weeks ago." Upon seeing her distressed features he took her hand in his. "She's okay—truly she is. She suffered no permanent effects, and the doctors have her on a powerful drug therapy. Nevertheless they asked me to contact you in the Congo, and that's when I heard the news."

"Oh, how awful." Becky looked anxiously at him. "Are you sure she's all right?"

"Positive."

"I'll call them tonight." Her hands grew clammy at the thought. "Do they know you've come to Bay Island?"

He nodded. "They asked me to come."

Becky sat woodenly for moments. Everything was happening too fast. Michael—her parents. Emotions exploded within her—anguish, anger, trepidation. Disjointed sections of her life were colliding together, and the result could only be an explosion; she could feel it in every painful breath.

"And I'm going to need a place to crash tonight," he added, giving her a hopeful look.

"You're staying?" she exclaimed in disbelief.

"You didn't think I would travel almost three thousand miles for a twenty-minute conversation, did you?" he answered with a wry smile. "I plan to stay a few days. Do you have an extra bedroom?"

She shook her head violently. "You can't stay here, Michael!"

"Oh, it's like that, is it?"

Becky's heart went cold. "Yes, it is like that."

He lifted her chin with one hand and looked down at her, his gray eyes amused and hardly repentant. "I didn't mean to offend. I'm sorry if I did." He stood up. "Maybe you can direct me to a hotel." He paused. "They do have a real hotel on the island, I presume?"

"We have two hotels," she answered in distraction. "There are also condos and several bed and breakfast establishments to choose from. Being midweek, I'm sure you'll have your pick."

"One of the hotels will be fine." He reached into the inside pocket of his jacket and brought out an electronic date book. Quietly he worked the screen before finally speaking. "We'll have dinner tonight and discuss the next couple of days."

"Days?"

He cocked his brow at her, and she knew without a doubt he was laughing at her. "Yes, I believe we just had that discussion." He laughed. "You look shell-shocked, my dear. Maybe you need to finish that nap of yours once you escort me into town to find the hotel."

How easily he manipulated his requests to make a polite refusal impossible. He'd evidently perfected the skill during her absence and wasted no time using it to his advantage, but to what purpose? What was his agenda?

"You can follow me in the cart," she suggested, trying to gain some control. When he didn't argue, she gathered her purse and swung it over her shoulder. The keys jingled nervously in her hands.

He was already to the door. "Lead the way."

She stepped out into the sunshine, and he followed. Leaning past him, she locked the door. "I think you'll like the Baymont Hotel, and it's not very far. We'll be turning right onto Shoreline Drive," she explained, pointing to the barely visible road. To her dismay she saw a familiar police cruiser turning off that very road toward Piney Point.

"I'll just follow you." He was already moving to the steps.

But Becky stood stock-still, and with butterflies in her stomach she watched Michael go down the stairs with non-chalant grace before glancing back at the road again. "This can't be good!" she said quietly.

Suddenly he turned. "Are you coming?" Obviously seeing her distraction, he slid his gaze to her line of vision then back to her. "Ah, your local gendarme. Promise—I'm clean." He laughed, pointing to the golf cart. "The little hootenanny's paid up."

Becky finally sprang to action and made her way down the steps. She'd better head off Michael. Who knew what Michael might say? She blew out a sigh. This was inconvenient. Not that she thought she could shuffle Michael off the island in a few days without anyone taking notice. Reports of the newcomer would spread far and wide before nightfall. It might be just as well to have Larry meet him first before the rumors had time to touch ground.

The white cruiser braked to a stop beside the four-seater cart, and Larry stepped out, his tall frame barely clearing the door opening.

"Good afternoon!" Larry greeted them both, but Becky could see his attention was focused on Michael. He left the engine running and made no move to close the door but leisurely moved toward them.

"Officer." Michael boldly stepped out and shook Larry's hand. "Michael Petit."

"Larry Newkirk," Larry responded with a pleasant but reserved tone, his facial expressions imperceptible as he peered from Michael to Becky.

"Larry, what a nice surprise," Becky managed, stepping forward. "What brings you by this afternoon?"

This seemed to prompt Michael to continue. "So you know each other then. What a relief that is," he said with a charming smile. "For a moment there you had me going." Becky could tell from his tone he hadn't been worried in the least. "Rebecca's kindly invited me to stay on the island for a few days."

Larry arched his eyebrow but said nothing. Becky flung Michael a warning glance only to receive a grinning, challenging look. Plainly he was enjoying the scene and, having sensed her distress, planned to make the most of it. This concerned her further. Had he always been like this? What she remembered as hard strength and decision—could it have been control? Had she been so immersed in her perceived love for him that she overlooked the obvious signals? Well, she determined, if he thought he could barge back into her life and easily maneuver her and those around her, he would soon find out otherwise.

"Larry," she finally said, pushing an easy smile to her lips. "I'm glad you stopped by so you could meet Michael. He's a dear childhood chum who decided to visit at the last minute." Her confidence rose a notch, and she reveled in the sudden start in Michael's face at her contradiction. "Matter of fact, I was just getting ready to escort him to the Baymont so he could find a room. But you know what?" She paused for the right effect and smiled at Larry. "Since you're making rounds, would you mind giving him an escort?"

"I wouldn't mind at all."

She turned to Michael. "You wouldn't mind, would you, if Larry took you in?"

Michael seemed speechless.

Larry gave Becky a knowing smile. "We're always glad to have new tourists on the island, and the Baymont is our finest hotel."

Becky could have kissed him. "But where are my manners?" she continued her charade. "You came here for a purpose. Is there something I can do for you?"

"I stopped by to remind you of the camp meeting at seven."

"Oh, I almost forgot," she remarked truthfully and after a moment turned to Michael. "I'm sorry, Michael, but we'll have to postpone dinner—unless you care to eat early." One thing she could count on—Michael never ate before seven.

"No, that's all right," he answered with resignation.

"Maybe tomorrow night. I'll call you." She turned to Larry. "Thanks for seeing him safe and sound to the hotel. You're a gem."

"No problem."

"See you at seven then?"

"Seven o'clock."

She turned to Michael, finally giving him some attention. "Have a good evening, Michael." She gave him a charming smile, but their gazes met and clashed. She would be in for a bad quarter of an hour once he would be free to talk with her. She'd turned the tables on him, and he wouldn't like that one bit.

Michael pulled out his hundred-dollar sunglasses and casually slid them on before plopping himself into the golf cart. Larry took the cue and made his way back to the car.

Becky didn't move until Larry had pulled the cruiser out and Michael turned the golf cart around to follow. They disappeared into the distance. It took several minutes before she turned and made her way up the steps. Still shaken by Michael's sudden appearance, she wondered what his visit would do to her already unsettled life. One thing she knew: Michael would not be given a length of leash to lead her about. She was no longer the same woman, and in some sense she was no longer alone. She had Larry!

seven

Larry shifted in his seat and settled in to listen as Jason Levitte spoke about possible dates for the Thunder Bay groundbreaking ceremony. His mind, however, kept drifting to the raven-haired beauty sitting next to him. Her silky black mane, pulled into a smooth ponytail, hung lightly over the back of the chair, and her loosely balled fist propped her delicate chin. She seemed quite absorbed by the topic and oblivious to his unfocused attention or frequent glances.

Having come late to the meeting, she'd successfully dodged any conversation beyond a nod of greeting. Not that she'd be inclined to talk after the meeting, especially if it concerned the unexpected arrival of her male friend to the island. Off limits! She might not say it in so many words, but he knew. She didn't talk about family, and she most certainly wouldn't be disposed to converse about the man she seemed so anxious to pawn off earlier that afternoon. He just hoped the new visitor wouldn't keep her from their needed duties. Once the date was set for the groundbreaking, they would have more work to do than either of them could handle.

"May first then?" Jason asked, and the room grew quiet.

Looking at Jason and then to the rest of the committee members, Larry realized they were waiting on him to answer. "May first?" he repeated, flipping the page of his planner over a month. "I'm on patrol in the late afternoon, but during the day it looks clear."

"What about the May Day celebrations?" It wasn't surprising Mr. Edwards's first contribution to the meeting was a question. His modus operandi was to begin with a question before an onslaught of biased opinions. "No, sir, that date won't do.

There will be the parade and all those newfangled carnival events. Why, the island will be crawling with people."

"That's true," Jason remarked. "You might have missed the earlier discussion about the May Day celebration and how we can use the events to our advantage."

Of course Larry bristled. They'd discussed the May Day celebration earlier. Mr. Edwards was too busy yakking in Culliver's ear to hear the discussion. Culliver was as deaf as they came, and neither seemed the least bit disturbed that the others had difficulty hearing over their loud voices. But Jason was cool as ever, and Larry wondered, not for the first time, why Jason hadn't gone into law enforcement instead of architecture—other than the fact he was a top-notch designer and easily pulled down four times as much income. Yet it wasn't the brilliant designs or ample bank accounts Larry desired; it was Jason's patience. He had a way with people. Larry had worked hard over the past year to develop more staying power and tolerance—to use these enduring life skills not only at work but in his personal life as well.

He tapped the pen between his fingers lightly on the table. His patience would always be a work-in-progress as long as Mr. Edwards stuck around to stretch his reserves.

"If we schedule the groundbreaking for eleven o'clock," Jason continued, "we'll be able to catch the crowd before the noon kickoff. This will be a good boost not only for the camp but for the landmark itself. As a committee we should do everything we can to promote the landmark in appreciation to Kelly Enterprises." He looked around the room at the other members. "The church calendar is clear, and most, if not all, committee members are available."

"I could work on setting up a booth for free refreshments," Becky chimed in. "If we want to attract as many islanders and visitors as possible, refreshments are a general magnet." She penned a flurry of notes in her notebook. "I'll see about helium balloons for the kids. Flora at the Balloon Boutique might be willing to donate several dozen."

Larry watched the hopeful expressions chasing each other across her mobile face with some amusement. "Good idea!" he encouraged. "There's a canvas canopy tent in the church garage we can use and an old but working helium tank if we need more balloons. Harvey can fill the tank for next to nothing." He looked to Jason. "We should also have fliers about our camp to pass out."

"We'll work on that!" Lottie BonDurant looked at Mrs. Phillips, who nodded in agreement.

"Thank you, ladies," Jason responded, smiling at the duo.

"Let's have a vote on the date." Larry proposed. "If Becky believes we can pull this together in three weeks, I say we go for it."

Becky turned slightly to see him. "We should be ready!"

Jason looked over at Mr. Edwards. "What's your call?"

"I suppose." Something short of a growl accented his reluctant approval.

Mr. Edwards never gave in easily, but Larry was glad he'd agreed without a twenty-minute dissertation. Jason followed with a vote, and the meeting adjourned. Larry watched as Becky closed her notebook and stood, sliding the heavy, leather chair back into place. He heard the arms of her chair thud against the table as he began to rise. Their gazes met.

"What do you think about having the high school pep band perform at the opening?" Becky was asking him.

He lifted his eyebrows in thought. "The marching band is usually in the May Day kickoff, and the pep band members are probably in the marching band." Before she would think him a pessimist again, he agreed to ask the school. "Don't be disappointed if they aren't able to come. There can't be more than twenty-five band members as is, so separating the pep band won't be an option."

She appeared satisfied and walked quietly beside him as they exited the building. "I hope you didn't mind showing Michael to the hotel this afternoon. Afterward I thought it was awfully pushy of me."

"I was glad to do it," Larry responded. "He isn't a very talkative fellow, though, is he? He did manage to say he was from Sacramento." He slid a look her way. "Hope he's settling in all right. He didn't seem quite satisfied with the hotel." He paused. "I get the impression the simple Baymont wasn't his usual style."

"He'll get over it!"

Something in her tone prevented him from pursuing the matter. She'd say no more; that much he knew. As predicted, this friend of hers was off-limits. Larry would risk his badge the newcomer from Sacramento was the author of the letter she'd received the other day. The correspondence had troubled Becky before she'd even opened the envelope and could account for the less than warm reception her childhood chum had been given. And the man had all the marks of a rich jet-setter. This was yet another puzzle piece of her past she seemed unwilling to discuss. There would be no more talking tonight.

Then she surprised him.

"You want to go for an ice cream at the Dairy Barn?" she suddenly asked.

"Okay," came his slow answer. What he really wanted to do was go home and hit the sack. The extra hours and rotating shifts were taking a toll. He perceived, though, that Becky's spur-of-the-moment invitation entailed more than an enjoyable outing. Avoidance perhaps? And if so, who else but her visiting friend could be the cause? The question begged to be answered—why should she want to avoid this Michael character?

They stopped at her borrowed car, and Becky threw her purse across and onto the passenger seat. "I'll meet you there."

Larry gave her a salute and walked to his truck. Less than a mile later he pulled into the lot and parked next to the small car. Falling in step beside her, they walked into the shop.

"What's your pleasure?" he asked her as they peered over the concaved, clear glass to the wide array of ice cream tubs. "The pecan-and-praline looks good."

With her lips pursed in contemplation she edged toward the second bin. "Well," she said, "what about the monthly special?"

Larry looked at the marked tub and wrinkled his nose. "Are you sure?"

"Heavenly Surprise is too intriguing to pass," she said with an amusing smile. "Have you no adventure?"

"Adventure, yes—death wish, no."

She laughed. "Chicken."

"Foods with the words *surprise* or *mystery* are generally named that way for a reason." He nodded to the clerk. "One scoop of pecan-and-praline, please." Unknown mixtures were right up there with chocolate cheese and pickled green beans.

Becky rolled her eyes at him before turning to make her order. "Make it the special for me."

"Ever heard the saying, 'better safe than sorry'?"

She laughed again. "What about, 'no pain, no gain'?"

"About midnight you'll be recalling that very saying, I'm sure." Larry took his napkin-wrapped cone and passed it to Becky while he reached for his wallet.

"Oh, no!" she protested. "I asked you out for ice cream."

"What are you going to do about it?" he responded, pointing to the cones she held in each hand. "Someone on the camp committee has to treat you right so you don't quit from a lack of appreciation." He took the change and slid the coins into his front pocket.

She frowned at him as he took his cone from her hand, but he could tell she was pleased. "Next time, my treat."

"I'm glad to hear it. Next time I'll order a triple."

They walked outside and sat on the red-painted bench of a picnic table.

She twirled the cone and murmured her approval as she took a 360-degree swipe of ice cream. "A triple it is—as long as you order the special. It's really good." She tipped her cone toward him. "Want to try it?"

"Absolutely not!" he exclaimed, playfully holding his hand over his chest. "What if you have tuberculosis or whooping cough—or something worse? You trying to kill me?"

She shook her head. "Oh, I can't afford to lose you. Who else will keep my feet grounded on the camp project? Besides, we have those issues of water and electricity to work on." She looked at him. "And your ice cream's melting."

Larry could feel the cool, sticky wetness dripping across his fingers. "It's all your fault," he announced, quickly taking in the drippings. "If you hadn't chosen that awful flavor and then offered to kill me with it."

"Has anyone ever mentioned you're hopeless?"

"Hopeless?" He tilted his head. "Not lately. But I'm sure if I stick around you long enough, the term will come up now and again."

She smiled. "I don't doubt it."

They ate their cones in companionable silence for several minutes. Conversation turned to the May Day groundbreaking before their dialogue dwindled into nothing. Larry wadded the wet and sticky napkin into a ball and looked up. Dusk had overtaken the sky.

He took a lungful of the night air. "Ready?"

"I guess." She made no attempt to move.

Larry altered his position to look at her more, instantly sensing her reluctance to leave. "Do you need me to see you home?"

"No, thanks."

"Is everything okay?"

She nodded and turned her gaze to the emerging stars above. "I'd probably better go back to Piney Point before it gets too late. I have a few phone calls to make." There was a lack of enthusiasm in her voice.

"Come on," he urged. "I'll at least see you to your car." He stifled a yawn.

She gave a pained smile and said softly, "I'm sorry." She stood to her feet. "You're probably bushed and have to be up and about early in the morning. Here I am keeping you out late listening to me ramble on about nothing."

"I don't need much sleep." He wanted to kick himself for letting her see his tiredness. "If you're not ready to go back. . ."

"No, I'm ready," she said with what he would call resignation.

They walked side-by-side to her car. The warmth of the day had lifted, leaving a clammy cool in its place, and he saw her give a slight shiver. Her pale, bare arms reflected from the overhead light, and he wished he had a jacket to give her.

"Thanks for the ice cream." Becky lifted her head and regarded him steadily. "I owe you one."

"I won't let you forget."

She stopped by her car and gave a half smile. "I'm sure you won't."

He opened the car door and firmly closed it when she settled into the driver's seat. "Buckle up and be careful," he warned then backed away. He waited until she pulled out of the parking lot before climbing into his truck. Her reluctance set his mind to wondering about her Sacramento friend. Was he the cause of her hesitation? Did she worry he'd be waiting for her?

He pulled the truck out of the lot and made his way around Shore Lane, slowing as he passed the road leading to Piney Point. In the emerging moonlight he could see her parked car and no other vehicles.

"Help the young lady out, God," Larry spoke aloud. "I don't know what's eating her, but she looked worried tonight. Show her Your peace."

Satisfied, he drove home and welcomed a night of un-interrupted sleep.

❧

Becky twisted her hands together as she paced in front of the unlit fireplace. Her eyes shifted to the silent phone, and she shook her head. No, she wasn't ready. It would take a few more minutes before her nerves would settle enough to make her move.

Becky thought back over the night. Larry had been such a gentleman. To be honest she didn't think he really wanted to go for ice cream. What a knucklehead she'd been. Of course the man was exhausted. She'd seen the barely concealed yawn. He worked a full-time, stressful job between offering his handyman services, and added into the mess was the camp business. Since Jason's return the two of them had been busy with permits, zoning, and variances.

A smile lit her lips. If possible, the man was becoming better looking every time she saw him. The well-shaped head on wide shoulders; the laughing blue eyes, piercing and intelligent; the firm jawline and well-defined mouth told her he was made of strong stock. She might even let her mind dream a bit—no, no, and no! Her time and resources were limited and unknown. What if she let herself fall for him? Or worse—what if he fell for her?

The abrupt *clang* of the ringing phone caused her to jump, knocking the chair into the table at her side. With a pounding heart she stood still staring at the offending noise. She wouldn't answer it! Most assuredly it was Michael. The phone rang off and on all afternoon, and she hadn't answered it then—she wouldn't now. She was in no mood to listen to what she knew was coming—his predictable ranting about his earlier dismissal. She needed all her energy to prepare herself for talking with her parents.

The phone finally grew silent, and she gave it a dubious look.

The thought of lifting the phone receiver and dialing the familiar number nearly made her nauseous. It was ridiculous really! She was a grown woman after all. They were her parents and no longer could lord over her, unleashing their venom unless she gave them permission to do so. She'd overcome many obstacles in life. God had strengthened her during her time in the Congo, teaching her more in a year than she could have understood in a decade in the States. She was a woman of God, not a woman of fear.

Taking a deep breath, she marched to the phone and lifted the receiver. With determined fingers she punched the numbers in quick succession. A brief pause followed with ringing—and ringing. Eleven, twelve, thirteen—no answer. Holding the receiver briefly to her chest, she dropped it back into place, letting a relieved breath escape as she dropped herself against the wall. Reprieved! Not even the dreaded answering machine to do business with. The firing squad was disbanded for yet another day.

Hoisting herself away from the wall, she switched on the kitchen light. Suddenly she was hungry for a ham and cheese sandwich. Tomorrow would deal with itself. After a good night's sleep she would have the strength to deal with Michael and her parents.

"You are the remarkable God who makes the weak strong!" she announced toward heaven with certainty.

She opened the refrigerator and peered inside at the wide array of food before slowly letting the door close. A refrigerator! What an amazing appliance. What a shock to adjust to life without one. But she had done it.

A sudden and overwhelming sentiment caused her heart to lurch. She didn't want to be here in a warm kitchen with a full refrigerator when the ones she loved were living without. Contentment seemed so fickle, so relative to each person's wants. Even the small grocery store on the island, the one mainlanders called quaint, represented a bonanza-style of offerings never, ever seen by the Congolese people. When she first came to the island, she remembered with shame how she'd complained about the lack of variety compared to the megastores where she'd shopped in California. *God, forgive me! What a spoiled lot Your people have become. Contentment isn't relative to my life or those around me, but to You. The fullness of life's blessings can only be enjoyed when shared with others.*

Her heart ached. How she longed to be back in the Congo.

Becky slid to the floor, feeling the slickness of the wood cabinets against her back. What if God didn't let her return? Would she ever feel whole again?

"You've given me so much," she prayed aloud. "I'm having a go at it trying to adjust back to the status quo, but You don't want me there, do You? I want to appreciate everything You've given me and not take for granted the blessings which never stop." She laughed. "Even the ice cream tonight was such a treat. I wish I could have shared it with Yelessa and Regine."

A tear trickled down her cheek. "I'm worried. Why hasn't word come yet about their well-being? You will protect them, won't You? I know You can. But what I'm really asking is—will You?" She shook her head. "No, what I'm asking for is their protection, if You can be glorified through that. What an awesome God You are. Teach me. Show me what You want from me. Make it clear. Sometimes I'm too dense to see Your path. Give me the simple version—the God's-Will-for-Dummies version."

Why did she feel so emotionally overwhelmed? It wasn't big setbacks or problems making her loss feel more acute, but the small, insignificant things of life—the smell of a wood-burning fire, the ratty towels in Larry's truck, or the taste of tropical fruit. She'd listened to other missionaries speak about the emotional turmoil associated with reentering the United States, leaving behind one culture for another. But she'd only been in the Congo for a year. Surely she could adapt for the short time she would be here. At times she felt normal; then a sudden, overpowering sensation would strike her very being, driving her mind back to the people she loved while her body remained trapped, chained to the life she now lived.

Yet. . .she enjoyed Bay Island and working with Larry. What a confused mess she was!

Becky drew up her knees and rested her chin. Was she going

crazy? How could her mind and soul be split between two lives at the same time? Adding to the heap, Michael's arrival on the island with messages from her parents caused a collision of yet another culture.

She was emotionally spent. Yet she knew God could and would renew her spirit—starting with a good night's sleep.

Grabbing the countertop, she pulled herself to standing. A deep sigh seemed to drain the last of her energy. Abandoning the plans for a ham and cheese sandwich, she switched off the light. Her feet padded down the hallway and into the bedroom. Changing into a gown, she collapsed into the bed, closed her eyes, and let her burdened heart drift into sleep.

eight

Becky toyed with the toast on the blue-flowered china plate. Although she slept deep and hard, morning arrived much too soon. In a daze she watched the warm, narrow shaft of light skitter across the counter and spray light through her water glass, refracting tiny rainbows of colors on the toast.

A knock at the screen door broke her sleepy trance.

"It's Tilly here," announced her neighbor loudly through the screen. "You up for a visit?"

"Coming." Becky sauntered from the kitchen to the door with a smile and unhooked the latch. "Come on in."

Tilly stepped inside. "Don't mind if I do."

"You're around and about early this morning."

"Just checkin' to see how you're doing." She stopped and gave Becky a sharp look. "And I'd say you look as though you've not been sleeping too well."

"I'm sleeping okay," she answered. "It's taking awhile for my body to adjust to the time change." She waved Tilly to follow her to the kitchen. "How about sharing some toast for breakfast?" Popping two more slices of bread in the toaster, she pointed to the coffeepot. "I can make some if you'd like. I'm not much of a coffee drinker, but this morning a cup might give me the jump start I need."

"That new young fella keep you out late?" Tilly asked without fanfare, eyeing her. "And, yes, I'd like some coffee if you're makin' a batch."

Becky hesitated a moment before sliding the carafe from the coffeemaker and walking to the sink. "Now how do you know about a certain young man?"

"Fred at the Cart Corral, of course," Tilly answered. "That

new fella asked after you when he rented the cart. Said he was a close friend of yours, he did. Fred didn't like 'im too much, though, and wouldn't tell 'im, but his wife, Mirabelle, couldn't help herself and told 'im anyways."

Becky remained silent as she went about pouring water into the coffeemaker and stuffing a white filter into the brown bucket.

"I see you're not sayin' much." A smile broke out on Tilly's round face. "Couldn't get much out of Larry either."

The mention of Larry's name grabbed Becky's attention, and she stopped midair with a scoop of coffee crystals. "Larry?"

"He's on early patrol this mornin'," Tilly was saying. "I flagged him down to see how the camp project was comin' along. He's real talkative about the camp but tight-lipped as can be about your visitor."

Becky dropped three more scoops into the basket. "A discreet cop! I knew there was something I liked about Larry." In went another scoop. "What did he say about the camp?"

"Quite an earful actually." Tilly stopped and pointed to the coffeemaker. "You keep it up and both sets of our eyeballs will be rollin' back into our heads."

"Oh!" Becky halted and looked into the nearly full basket. She scooped out several spoonfuls. "So what did he say about the camp? Is he happy with the project?"

"Tickled pink, I'd say," she replied. "He did say old Edwards was givin' you a hard time. That's another reason why I came over—to make sure the old coot doesn't scare you off." She tossed Becky a look. "Plus Larry asked me to check on you."

"Check on me?" This alerted Becky like a prod in the ribs.

"I'm only tellin' you what he said." She shrugged her large shoulders. "He's a caring body, that's for sure." Several more praises followed until Becky thought she'd laugh aloud.

"It's useless, Tilly," she murmured, trying to hide her smile. "I know Larry's a great guy. The problem is, I'm not available."

Tilly drew her brows together in concern. "It's that young fella who came yesterday, is it?"

"No." It wasn't any of Tilly's concern, but Becky took no offense. She knew the motherly woman meant no harm. In some ways it felt comforting to know someone cared enough to notice even the small particulars of her life. There was a reason why Tilly was well loved by the island residents—her own love of people.

"Someone else?"

"There's no one else," she assured Tilly. "And before you start pairing Larry and me together, it's only fair to tell you he's not interested in me that way. We're working together, that's all."

"Uh-huh," Tilly grunted. "I've been around the block enough times to know when a fella's interested in a woman. And he sure does ask about your well-being enough to make a body wonder."

Becky tossed Tilly a dubious glance and poured two cups of coffee. "He might be worried that I'm offended by Mr. Edwards, as you said before. But Larry can stop worrying. It's okay—really it is."

This seemed to derail Tilly from her matchmaking mission for a moment. "Old Edwards is a real sweetheart down deep."

"Really?"

"Really!"

Becky took a sip of coffee and felt an instantaneous jolt. Her eyes began to water. "You might need some sugar and cream for this coffee," she pronounced at once, scooting over the sugar bowl and shoveling in several teaspoons. "Wow!"

"Just right!" Tilly said, taking a big gulp without flinching. "But like I was sayin', Van can be a real softie once you get to know him."

"His name is Van?" This tidbit amazed Becky. "I don't think I've ever heard him being referred to by his first name. Like Mrs. Phillips, it's almost as if they don't even have first names." She shoved the overpowering coffee cup to the side. "Mr. Edwards seems to be passionate about the camp project, but at times it's difficult to know whether he's for or against the camp. He resists nearly every move that's made. Surely he can see how God has provided in ways we could never have expected."

Tilly smiled. "He's from the old school. But if you can prove your point of view with facts that make sense to him, he'll be behind you one hundred percent. And he's one good ally to have."

"You seem quite fond of him."

To Becky's surprise the older woman blushed a light pink. "He's been at the church for more years than I care to remember, that's all." She smoothed the folds of her light blue checked dress with her hands. "He can come off being a bit harsh, and I'd hate to see you takin' it the wrong way—hard feelings and all."

"I'm not the one he needs to worry about. Lottie almost decked him the other night," Becky proclaimed with some amusement. "He started an exposition on the roles of women versus men."

Tilly shook her head. "It'll do him no good gettin' Lottie all riled up." She drained the last of her cup. "I might call the old coot and have a heart-to-heart with him. Someone needs to keep him in line."

"If anyone can do it, it's you." Becky laughed.

Tilly winked at her. "I'm takin' that as a compliment.

"Such is the spirit in which it was said."

Tilly stood. "I'd better skedaddle and get to my chores." She gave Becky a level look. "And you'd better get you some sleep. Don't let that young fella keep you out to all hours gallivantin' across the island. You look a might peaked and need your rest."

"Yes, Tilly."

"I can have Larry check on you later if there's something you need—"

"No," Becky nearly shouted. "I'm fine! Really." She had her

hands full enough dealing with Michael's presence; she didn't need an audience—especially Larry.

"All right then." Tilly made her way to the door. "Take care of yourself now, and call on ol' Tilly if you need anything."

"I will."

Tilly clomped down the outside steps, and Becky latched the door before making her way back to the kitchen. She dumped the coffee in the sink and moved the toaster back into place. It was then she saw the untoasted bread sitting idle in the machine. It did little good to place bread inside the appliance if it wasn't plugged in.

The neglected bread was much like her, she reasoned with some anxiety. If Tilly knew about Michael, then so did half the community. What a thought that was. She'd better keep Michael unplugged from the local gossip—or she'd be toast.

❧

Becky watched as Michael strolled up the narrow walk to the café. The small bell above the entrance jingled as he opened the door and breezed through the opening. He searched the room until their gazes met and quickly weaved between the tables until reaching her.

"Why are you sitting so far back?" he asked, taking off his sunglasses. "Any further back and we'll be doing dishes."

Becky motioned for him to sit across from her. "It will give us some measure of privacy so we can talk." She wouldn't dare let him know the back booth would also limit the prying eyes she wished to avoid at all costs.

"I don't know why we couldn't have met at the hotel," he insisted as he slid across the maroon vinyl seat. He gave the room a cursory look. "The hotel restaurant is more than a step or two above this joint."

Becky took two menus from the holder at the end of the table and extended one to him. "They have good food. You won't complain, I promise."

He cast her a skeptical glance before looking over the

menu. Both decided on soup and a sandwich. He frowned when the waitress informed him the establishment did not serve alcoholic beverages. Brusquely he ordered a mineral water and said nothing until the waitress returned with their drinks.

"You know," Michael finally began, resting his arm on the back of his seat, "I'm not exactly happy with the stunt you pulled yesterday. Being made to look like a fool wasn't in the plans for our happy reunion." He took a leisurely swallow of his cold drink. "You have something going on with that police guy or what?"

Becky watched the turbulence made by her spoon as she stirred her iced tea. The action gave her time to think, time to pray for guidance. Much-needed ground rules would have to be set. "Michael," she finally began, drawing a deep breath, "you can't just plummet from the sky after two years and expect me to drop everything. I am glad to see you. Truly I am." She hesitated. "But I can't let you take over like you're used to doing. I'll try to be as flexible as I can while you're here."

He looked both surprised and hurt. "That doesn't seem quite realistic. When have I ever tried to take over?"

She had to smile at his naiveté. "You've always been a leader, Michael. And up until two years ago I deferred to your judgment of where we should eat, where we should go, or even which college classes to take."

"That's hardly taking over," he said, drawing his brows together.

"Don't be offended, Michael," she gently pleaded. "I didn't mind back then. You always took good care of me. But things are different now."

"Different?" He gave her a long, steady look. "In what way are things different?"

Becky pushed back her hair. "It's hard to explain."

"Try me!"

"My focus in life has changed drastically in the past two years. The Congo is incredibly different from anything I've ever experienced."

"Because they're impoverished?"

She nodded. "That's part of it, I suppose. These people live, and have lived their whole lives, without anything we'd call of worth. I had to adapt to their way of living. It was difficult to adjust at first—to change how I dressed, how I ate, how I slept—how I related to people. Most of all I had to adjust to being alone with God. Here in the States I'd come to depend heavily on my job, my bank account, and even my friends. But when that's all stripped away, what do you have?" She spread her hands out. "God!"

"Certainly they didn't send a single woman out in that wilderness alone?" He seemed taken aback by such an idea.

"No," she answered, flustered that she couldn't adequately describe her experience of faith. "Another missionary couple was serving in the next village to help me. What I'm trying to say is, I'm different because God has let me rely on Him without the aid of my usual safety nets."

Michael gave her an uncomprehending look. "I'm sure such an experience would broaden one's view of the world, but what does that have to do with you and me and my visit?"

"For one thing," she said, "I'll be returning to the Congo once it's safe again."

"Safety is a fickle thing in those countries. It wouldn't be wise to go back for a long, long time." His brows drew together. "You don't already have a date set to return, I hope!" he exclaimed with a flash of alarm in his eyes.

"No." She shook her head. "It's a wait-and-see situation right now."

"That's good—very good." He thoughtfully rubbed his chin. "So what you're telling me is that God has shown you how to be selfless and how to make a difference in people's lives." Michael's face broke out into a smile. "That can't be much different from the Becky I knew before." He reached across the table and took both her hands in his. "You never had a selfish bone in your body. Don't you know it was your selflessness that attracted me to you in the first place? If this God-thing improved your attributes I'm all for it, because it's only made you better, not different."

Other people were drifting into the café. They cast interested glances toward them, and Becky lightly pulled her hands out of his grasp.

She tilted her head back. "Can I ask you a question?"

"Of course."

"Why did you come to Bay Island?"

He seemed bewildered. "I think you know the answer to that question—to talk with you." His eyebrows lifted. "Why does that surprise you?"

"You could have phoned to talk with me."

He nodded. "I suppose that's true. It wouldn't have taken much effort to get your number." He shrugged expressively. "I wanted to see you in person."

Becky's heart turned over. "But why?"

"When I heard you might be in danger, it did something to me. I don't know." He paused a moment. "We didn't part on the best of terms when you left, and I'm afraid I must take responsibility. I shouldn't have pushed you." He leaned forward. "As I said before, I came to talk with you about your parents; but I suppose I've also come to see if anything was left of our relationship."

Becky could feel the blood drain from her face. She'd never seen Michael so humble or brutally honest. And she was confused. "You realize the same issues still exist, Michael? My life is dedicated to doing what God wants of me. We don't share that same dedication."

"Cutting right to the chase, aren't you?" His gray eyes narrowed in deliberation. "I can live with your convictions about God. Do I have to believe exactly as you do? Not everyone is as gung ho as you are. We could learn to accept one another's positions."

Becky shook her head slowly. Michael was trying so hard, but he didn't have a clue what it meant to follow God. His idea of Jesus was limited to the making of a good story. He had no personal interest. "I know this is hard for you to understand, but God makes it clear that I can't seek a serious relationship with someone unless that person's focus is the same. It's more than having different tastes in furniture."

Michael flicked his glance over her face. "That's so. . . intolerant."

"God is intolerant at times."

He laughed. "That's the most absurd notion I've ever heard."

"Did God let the Israelites worship other gods?" she asked. "He did, but they suffered the consequences. God is jealous of anything that keeps us from doing what He wants."

"And you don't think a few thousand years has made a difference?" There was frustration in his voice.

"For both of our sakes, I hope not."

"And that means. . ."

"God doesn't change. His Word doesn't change," Becky continued, softening her voice when she noticed the rejection in the depths of his eyes. "God loves you, Michael Petit, and He wants you to accept Him as the driving force for everything you do. He sent His Son to die on the cross so you could have a direct connection with Him. But you have to make the move—not to please me, but to please God. It's not about church attendance or pledging money to the church— it's about you and God. He doesn't want your tolerance. He wants you!"

A painful silence followed until Michael straightened in his seat. "How did we move from exploring our relationship to preaching?" His mouth twisted into a half smile, but his eyes were determined. "I'm only here for a couple of more days. Can we spend some time together for old times' sake? I promise to be good if you promise to stay out of the pulpit."

"Well. . ."

The waitress arrived with their lunch, and Michael took the opportunity to move their conversation on. "Did you call your folks last night?"

She drew back, disappointed. She'd muffed it again. Would Michael never understand his soul was at stake?

"Well?" he prompted.

"I tried."

"Did you leave a message?"

"The answering machine never picked up," she explained. "I'll try again this afternoon."

He took a bite of sandwich. "You're not trying to avoid calling, are you? Your mother might not be in immediate danger, but she is extremely worried."

"I did try calling," she repeated. "Have you spoken with them since yesterday?"

He seemed reluctant to answer. "Yes. . .last night. I also tried calling you, but no one answered."

"I was at a planning meeting until late."

"With that police officer?"

"He's the head of the committee."

"That's convenient." Michael's egotistical behavior seemed to be seeping back.

"What's that supposed to mean?"

He gave her hand a quick, friendly squeeze. "Nothing at all. Let's not talk about your police friend anymore. How about we plan something for tonight? Would you like to take in a movie this evening?"

Becky shook her head. "We don't have a movie theater on the island."

"Then what do you do for fun around here?"

"Well," she began, "we're a little too old for the arcade, and it's too early in the season for midweek entertainment." She smiled. "But I could show you Thunder Bay."

"Thunder Bay?"

"It's an old Civil War site," she happily explained. "Property has been donated to build the camp on part of the land. I'd like you to see what I'm working on."

"All right," he said.

"How about six o'clock? We'll have plenty of light left in the day to see the place."

"Are you driving, or do you want me to pick you up in the hootenanny?"

She thought about this. Which would draw less attention? "We'll take your hooten—I mean your golf cart." What a mess! He had her talking like him.

He laughed. "I'll be there."

She smiled back then sobered. While she planned to share a visit to Thunder Bay with Michael, it was Larry who now drifted into her mind. It was Larry who shared her enthusiasm for the camp and her work. It was Larry she wanted to be with. Was her heart treading into dangerous territory without her permission? If Tilly was right in her observations, Larry might be in the same boat. The thought warmed her heart and yet made her head swim. Between Larry and Michael she was headed for trouble. What had she gotten herself into?

nine

Larry opened the door to his cruiser, grabbed his hat and ticket pad, and swung his long legs out. The leather of his black holster creaked when he stood, and he paused long enough to fit the police hat firmly over his crew cut. When would Walter Burchell stop parking his worn-out Cadillac across the street from the Schooner's Surf and Turf—right in front of the fire hydrant?

"I've parked in the same spot for thirty-some odd years," he'd said over the last ticket, "and I don't plan on changing."

It didn't matter to Walter that city water had been placed along Pelican Avenue ten years ago or that fire hydrants were a natural and welcome outcome. Walter insisted he'd been there first, not the water, and that was all there was to it.

Larry flipped open the citations book and thumbed through the pages until he found the next fresh sheet. Slowly he walked to the two-tone blue car and withdrew a pen from his shirt pocket. How many tickets would this make—nineteen, maybe twenty? It was as if the guy enjoyed personally funding the city coffers. He'd pay the ticket every time with plenty of lip service and behave for a short time, but it wasn't long before his car would find its way back to the usual spot. Just like now! Good thing parking tickets didn't rack up points against a driver's license like moving violations. Otherwise Walter would be walking.

Leaning over the windshield, Larry copied the vehicle identification number from the metal tag on the dash. *I should have it memorized by now.* It took a short time to fill in the remaining information. Finishing the sheet, he tore off the top copy and placed it snugly under the driver's side windshield wiper blade. He looked at his watch before heading back to the white cruiser. The leather bottoms of his shiny black uniform shoes ground against the small stones on the street. Only forty-five more minutes and he could call it a night. He'd agreed to cover an extra three hours for another officer, making for a long day. Seven o'clock couldn't come too soon.

His walkie-talkie radio came to life. "Dispatch to one-ninety-four."

Larry reached for the handheld mike clipped to the cloth epaulet on the left shoulder of his starched white shirt. Depressing the lever, he turned and leaned his head close to the mouthpiece. "One-ninety-four—Pelican and Ferry Avenues."

"One-ninety-four," announced the professional-sounding female voice coming across his walkie, "please respond to a ten-thirty-eight at the Thunder Bay Civil War Landmark, at six-two-five Runaway Bay Road. Meet caller at the rear of the property."

Larry felt a shot of adrenaline surge through his body. He squeezed the lever again. "Do we have a caller's name?"

"That would be an affirmative. I'll check the report." There was a brief silence. "The caller is a Becky Merrill."

"I'm on it! E.T.A. four minutes." Larry tossed his hat inside the cruiser and climbed inside. He didn't know what Becky Merrill could be doing at Thunder Bay at this hour or what property damage might have occurred, but he didn't like the sound of it.

"One-ninety-four," the dispatcher's voice continued to crackle across the line, "do you need a backup unit for that location?"

"Negative," he answered. "I'll check and advise."

Larry put the cruiser in gear. His foot felt heavy on the gas pedal as he pulled onto the road and made an immediate U-turn. He could hear stones hitting the undercarriage of the car as he accelerated. His mind computed the information given. Property damage to Thunder Bay would most certainly be related to one of the Civil War buildings, but he'd been directed to the rear of the property—the camp property.

The shoreline scenery passed, and he glanced at the speedometer. The digital numbers corresponded precisely with the posted speed limit, and he once again focused his attention and energy to the destination at hand. Soon Thunder Bay came into sight, and he pulled the cruiser to a stop at the entrance. He stepped out and twisted his hat back on. Laying a hand over the butt of his gun in a subconscious move, he strode up the path toward the outbuildings. Nothing looked amiss.

He pressed on toward the break in trees to the first back lot. He spotted two figures standing close together with their backs turned. It was Becky who turned first as he neared the couple.

Becky left the other figure and moved toward Larry with alacrity, greeting him with what he could only call relief. "Larry. I'm so glad you were still on duty. I thought you'd left for the day."

"What's the problem, Becky?" His glance diverted from her concerned face to the other person joining them, the man he now recognized as Michael from Sacramento. He acknowledged his presence with a polite nod before bringing his gaze back to Becky. "The dispatcher said you reported some type of property damage."

Becky touched his arm. "Come with me." She led him to the spot she'd just vacated. "Look at these." She made a wide sweep of her hands to the area in front of her. "There are dozens of holes dug throughout this part of the field. I'm sure it's not the work of an animal, but I can't imagine who or what it's from. I don't understand it at all."

Larry bent down and sat on his haunches to examine one of the holes. He pulled the heavy-duty flashlight from his utility holder, leaned on one knee, and shone the light into the dark depths. His black tie fell forward touching the ground. The hole was only eight to ten inches across, but a good two feet deep. On closer inspection he could see and feel the distinct ridges made from what he'd guess to be a posthole digger. Piles of fresh earth lay in a heap to the side.

"What do you make of it?" Becky was asking him.

Brushing off his hands, he stood. "I'd say someone's looking for something buried in the field. How many holes did you say there were?" He turned in a circle looking over the area, noticing several similar cavities and mounds of dirt.

"I'm not sure." She stood quite still, her voice sharp with distress. "Maybe thirty or forty of them."

"I'd say more like twenty-five," Michael offered, speaking for the first time.

Larry turned to look at him. "What time did the two of you arrive?"

"Not more than twenty minutes ago," he answered, flitting a glance at Becky. "Wouldn't you say that's right?"

"I suppose," she agreed with a nod. "I was showing Michael the land for the camp, and all of a sudden we noticed these holes." She was backing up to point behind Larry. "They start over there—"

Larry immediately shot his hand out and latched firmly onto her arm. "Watch it there." He pulled her forward from the yawning opening behind her. "You could easily break an ankle stumbling into one of these holes."

Startled, she turned to see the dark opening just inches from her feet. Even in the waning light Larry could see the light hue of pink highlighting her cheeks as he released his grip. She seemed breathless. "You're right, Larry. These are very dangerous. We'll have to fill them in tomorrow."

Larry nodded. "The two of you stay here and let me count the holes." He surveyed the area counting exactly twenty-five, just as Sacramento Michael had said. "Have you been over to the field next to the shore?" he asked Becky when he rejoined them again.

"We didn't see anything there," she responded. "We went to the back property first. It wasn't until we came back this way to see the pond that we found these holes."

"What do you think the person was looking for?" This question came from Michael.

Larry let his full gaze fall on the man beside Becky. He was the same height as he was but with a much different, stocky build and dark complexion. Not for the first time he wondered what relationship the two shared—or had shared. This much he noticed—Becky seemed almost to ignore her friend while fretting over the mysterious damage.

Finally Larry spoke. "My first guess would be the vandals are looking for old war relics since the holes are deep and narrow. If the person was looking to find a spot where several relics might be, they would pepper the area." He let his eyes scan the field. "There's almost an organized pattern."

Michael looked in the same direction. "You're probably right. The holes would have to be deep to find good Civil War items."

The man was smarter than he looked. "I'm working the afternoon shift tomorrow," he said to Becky. "I'll stop by early tomorrow morning and see what I can do about filling in these holes so someone doesn't get hurt. For now, I'll get my police tape and rope off the area."

"What time do you think you'll be here?" she asked. "I can meet you here."

Larry saw the frown creep across Michael's face, but the man said nothing. "I'm thinking about eight o'clock."

Becky nodded. "I'll be here."

"Why don't I pick you up?" Larry didn't know what prompted him to offer, but the suggestion must have been appreciated for he was rewarded with a big smile from Becky. "I'll walk you two out to the parking lot. I want to get the police tape put up before it becomes any darker."

The three made their way to the nearly vacant gravel lot.

Larry noticed the lone four-seater golf cart parked near the entrance and surmised it belonged to Becky's friend.

Suddenly he felt a warm hand on his arm. Becky was looking up at him. "Do you need help with the police tape? I could help."

"No. I'm fine." He looked at the golf cart again. "You'll be wanting to get back to Piney Point before dark settles in." Golf carts made great transportation—in the daytime, not at night. He could see Michael was already settling behind the wheel. "Make sure he uses the headlights."

"He will," she agreed after much hesitation, seeming reluctant to leave. "About a quarter till eight?"

"Quarter till eight," he repeated. "And don't worry about the holes. We'll take care of them tomorrow. It's probably a onetime deal. I doubt the vandals will be back."

"I sure hope so," she said in a low whisper.

Her worried tone caused him to give her a deeper look. "It will be okay," he assured her, giving her hand a light squeeze. "Trust me. You go on now and make sure you get a good night's sleep."

Becky nodded and gave a wave before heading for the golf cart. Larry opened the trunk of the cruiser and reached for the roll of police tape and four stakes.

"I thought we had breakfast plans in the morning," he heard Michael say after the white golf cart started and backed up several feet.

The cart moved away before Larry could hear Becky's response. He shut the trunk and walked back to the field. Placing the stakes and winding the tape around the irregular square perimeter gave Larry plenty of time to think. He couldn't put his finger on the problem, but Becky and her friend seemed—well, the closest he could describe was—uncomfortable. That was it. The two seemed uncomfortable. Becky didn't appear afraid, angry, or upset, but ill at ease. Much like last night when she asked him out for ice cream. He didn't know how concerned he should be or how involved he wanted to become. Tangling with females and their emotions could very well resemble a real minefield. Did he really want to go there?

Larry tied off the last of the tape. He supposed it was a good sign Becky liked to be with him, a point proven with her quick acceptance of a ride in the morning. Behind her bubbly, dreaming brain, however, were turbulent waters. Being yanked from the mission field could account for much of her troubles; yet his instincts told him there was much more. Something about Becky tugged on his sense of chivalry, and knowing her better would be a good thing; but she kept sending mixed signals. He didn't mind playing the white knight in shining armor as long as the damsel in distress wanted to be rescued. Having to drag a reluctant woman to safety put a genuine damper on the process.

Dark fell quickly, and he used his flashlight to navigate back to the cruiser. He sat behind the wheel and flipped on the interior light. It would take a few minutes to complete the report. He reached for the car radio mike, unclipping the mouthpiece from the holder. The coiled cord stretched easily.

"One-ninety-four to dispatch."

"Go ahead, one-ninety-four."

"The thirty-eight will be a code one."

"Copy."

"I'll be clear and code four and heading back to the station."

"Copy, one-ninety-four, and good night."

Larry looked at his watch. Seven forty-five! The police chief would have something to say about the overtime—again. Maybe he could bargain some comp time instead. He needed the time more than the money with the camp project moving forward on the fast track. Yes, the chief might be obliging. Anything to keep the dreaded overtime off the books.

ten

Becky sat stoically in the passenger seat, thankful for the warmth of her jacket as the cool wind whipped at her face and hair. Michael was angry with her. It was as though he believed she'd concocted the deep gopher-like holes as an excuse to avoid having breakfast with him.

She risked a glance at him. He sat beside her, his hands gripping the wheel of the golf cart while he gazed ahead as if seeing things beyond her vision. His profile, etched against the waning light, sent an odd shiver along her nerves. Suddenly he turned his head toward her as though aware of her scrutiny.

"Sure you won't reconsider breakfast tomorrow?" he asked for the second time. "I think your police friend could handle the job by himself. He looks strong enough. Besides, that type of manual labor isn't women's work. Any man worth his salt wouldn't let you help, let alone encourage your participation."

Becky only shook her head at his question and was relieved to see they were nearing Piney Point. Michael's mouth was pressed into a disagreeable line, and she'd about had enough for one day. He raced the cart up the incline and parked near the deck stairs then shut off the engine.

"What would it take to get you to California for a few days?" he asked abruptly, his gray eyes piercing her own.

Becky gave him a perplexed look. "California?"

"I want you to return with me to California," he explained. "Your parents are worried about you, and frankly I'm worried about you. This whole camp project—" He waved his hand in the air. "This camp project is stressing you out. I can see it in your face. What you need is some rest and relaxation."

"I can't just leave my duties, Michael. There's work to be

done, and the groundbreaking ceremony is just around the corner." His suggestion was ludicrous at best. "I'm going to try calling Mother and Father again tonight. They'll calm down once I let them know I'm all right."

"And when they find out their little girl is shoveling dirt—then what?" was his crisp reply. "Now tell me—what would it take to relieve you of these duties for a while? Ten thousand? Twenty?"

"Michael!" She couldn't believe her ears.

"Thirty?"

"Michael, stop it. I don't want your money."

"I wouldn't be giving it to you," he reasoned. "I'll donate the money to the camp so they can hire some island goon to dig trenches and backfill holes. There'd be enough to get someone else to do the piddly work they're running you ragged with."

Becky felt the air leave her lungs. Michael was being obstinate and unreasonable. He acted as though she didn't have the sense of a child. Did he believe throwing money at every problem he encountered would make the world a better place?

"Michael, the answer is no." She glared at him indignantly and stepped from the cart. "I don't want to go back with you to California. My home is here. And I don't want your. . .bribe money." She held onto the roof as she peered inside. "I like my job, and I'm good at it. Hard work never hurt anyone. There's no shame in manual labor."

Michael leaned over the passenger seat and stared up at her. "I'm not getting down on you, darling. I just care about what happens to you."

She drew back sharply. Darling? The endearment brought back memories and at the moment sounded contrived. "It's time to say good night, Michael. I'll call you sometime tomorrow."

"I won't be here."

"What's that supposed to mean?"

"I'm leaving after breakfast tomorrow," he announced. "I'd like you to come with me, but since you seem determined to work on this camp project, I'll just have to come back—with reinforcements."

Becky's hands shook. "Reinforcements?"

"When's this groundbreaking ceremony?" he asked, ignoring her startled gaze. "May first, is it? I'm not going to give up yet. Take care of yourself, Becky."

He started the engine and without further argument drove off, leaving Becky gaping after him. What nerve! She could hardly believe the audacity of the man. Reinforcements indeed! Who did he think he was? He couldn't just barge back into her life and take over.

With fervor she tromped up the steps and let herself into the cabin. Her keys clattered as she dropped them to the counter with more force than necessary. What impertinence! Her heart pounded in agitation, and a parallel, pulsating sensation could be felt above her left temple. It took several minutes to calm sufficiently to attack her next problem—her parents. Slowly she lifted the phone receiver and dialed the familiar number.

"Hello?" Her mother's voice came across the line, and Becky nearly buckled.

She held the phone tight to her ear. "Mother. . .it's Becky."

"Becky?" came the surprised gasp. "Is it really you?"

"Yes, it's really me."

"Are you all right?" her mother asked. "We've been extremely worried, you know. Is Michael there with you?"

Becky sank into the dining room chair. "I'm fine, and, no, Michael just left to go back to his hotel." She paused. "Michael told me you had a small stroke a few weeks ago. Is everything okay?"

"It was really nothing. The doctors have me on a blood thinner, and I have to watch my diet—that sort of thing." Becky could hear a sigh come across the line. "I think the stroke was more stress related, you know. Your father and I have been sick with worry about you since we heard about them pulling out the Americans. But what can you expect when you're living among savages? Who knows what could have happened to you?"

Becky set her teeth. The guilt-trip voyage was about to begin. "I was not living among savages, Mother."

But her mother wasn't listening. Becky could hear her talking to someone, and then her father's voice came across the line.

"Becky," boomed her father, "it's about time you gave us a call. Didn't Michael tell you how anxious we were? It's really inexcusable to keep us in such a state."

Becky rubbed one temple with her free hand. Michael said her parents' attitude had changed. How wrong could he be? It was as if their conversation picked right up from the day she left—their offensive attack, her defense.

"Daddy, I don't want to argue with you," she said gravely. "Michael said you were concerned and that you wished for me to call. I tried calling last night and this afternoon, but there was no answer and no answering machine to leave a message."

"We were home the entire evening last night," he said sharply. "Your mother could have been lying on her deathbed for all you care. Are you sure you weren't out all night with that police fellow Michael mentioned?"

This was going to get ugly. The old feelings of anger and disgust were rising like helium in her burning chest. Time had only scabbed over the wound, which refused to heal. If she didn't intervene, the old injury would break wide open.

"I won't argue with you, Daddy. You'll just have to take my word that I did call."

"Where's Michael?" came his crusty reply.

"At the hotel."

"You have him give me a call tomorrow," he demanded. "I want to talk with that boy."

"He's leaving in the morning," she answered. "If you want to talk with him, I suggest you give him a call tonight."

"Leaving?"

"That's what he told me a few minutes ago."

"Are you coming back with him?"

Becky felt constriction in her chest. Uncertainty clouded her voice, for a humiliating suspicion was taking form. "No."

"And why not?"

Coming back to California must have been her parents' idea, not Michael's. That had been the plan all along, but something caused Michael to make his move earlier than expected. This annoyed her immensely.

"No, I'm not coming back with Michael." She sat straighter in the chair. "I'm twenty-five years old and capable of taking care of myself. I'm not sure what Michael has told you, but I'm working on the island as a camp director until I have news on my position in the Congo. I realize you don't approve of the path I've chosen, but you must learn to accept who I am."

Her father grunted into the phone. "They've brainwashed you. That much I know."

"As I said before, I don't want to argue. I called to find out how Mother was doing. Can't we have a normal conversation?"

"You never did listen to your mother and me," he charged, and Becky could imagine the large vein on his forehead was bulging by this time. "You've always been strong-willed and difficult to raise. We've tried our best, and this is how we're rewarded? Your brother has a full-time job with a nationally known company and is earning what he's worth. If you had kept up your grades, you could have entered Stanford and by now—"

She interrupted his tirade. "Father?"

"What?"

"I do love you," she responded more calmly than she felt. "Tell Mother I love her, too. Thank you for sending Michael out to check on me, but you can stop worrying. I'm doing fine. I'll check on you and Mother again soon. Take care of yourselves, okay?"

With that she gently replaced the receiver. She'd taken control and stopped the vicious cycle she knew her father would have continued. God had given her the strength to bring the verbal abuse to an end. Then why did she feel so horrible? And why did she wish Larry were here to make things better. He would have known how to calm her father.

Larry! It was becoming more difficult to remain detached from his strengths—and his charms. He was solid as a rock and seemed to have a knack for fixing everything from water heaters to vandalism. Nothing moved him. Why then shouldn't he be an expert in fixing broken and tired hearts? And she was tired. Tired of fighting. Tired of setting a path of dreams and finding the path blocked. Tired of her parents. Tired of worrying about things she couldn't control. Larry would be the kind of man who could look at each problem with objectivity and help forge a plan of action. She needed his objectivity, and he could use a good dose of dreaming beyond static reality. What a combination they could make!

But she had the threat of rejection to consider. What would Larry say once he knew she came from the dreaded "talking money" background he detested? Or, worse yet, discovered her full-blown, bigger-than-life dysfunctional family was alive and well—and ready to interfere? It might be difficult for him to understand her family dynamics since she imagined his family to be idyllic.

There were so many ifs. *If* he was even interested in her. *If* he didn't turn tail and run when he found out about her family. *If* she were to remain on the island. *If* God didn't call her back to the Congo. *If* she could choose wisely. Hadn't she always heard women chose men who resembled their fathers? Oh, please. Don't let it be so!

And what did she know about men? She was too shy in high school and college to date anyone other than Michael. Her parents had said he was the right one for her and encouraged her to look no further—so she never did. That's what made it so laughable when Lauren had believed sometime ago that Becky and Jason were an item. Becky was working as Jason's bookkeeper when Lauren returned to the island. The whole thing was a big misunderstanding. If only Lauren had known the so-called beauty queen she feared was dateless and unavailable. Neither paid enough attention to realize.

Now there was Larry, the first man she'd felt comfortable with and the first man she'd consider sharing life experiences with. It scared her spitless.

God, give me wisdom to know Your path for my life. Life is hard, but I know You are good. Thank You for sending Larry. He's been a blessing. But I need help in navigating the waters—big time. Show this mixed-up woman what You want. Without You I'm toast!

❧

Larry pressed one heavy-duty boot back and forth over the freshly packed dirt. "That should do it."

"Wonderful!" Becky dusted the knees of her jeans with her hands and leaned on the shovel. "Let's hope whoever had the sudden urge to use this field for digging practice doesn't return."

"I'll make sure a few cars patrol this area regularly. It's unlikely the person or persons will return, but we won't take any chances." His look turned cautious. "Don't come out here alone, and if you're going to show it to your friend again, let me know. I don't want you to meet up with any intruders."

"Michael's already left the island."

Larry detected a tone—of what? Resignation, relief, or agitation? "I thought he was staying a few more days."

"Guess he had other things to do." She shrugged her shoulders. "It's just as well. I'm going to be busy this week setting up for the May Day groundbreaking."

Unfolding the blue tarp next to the cooler, he directed Becky to sit. "Let's take a water break before we clean up the tools."

Becky sat near the far corner. "Have you made much progress with the zoning variance?"

Larry rummaged through the cooler, took two water bottles in his hand, and extended one to her as cold water dripped off his fingers. "Council said there wouldn't be a problem. It's not like bigger cities where it takes an act of God to change zoning and obtain permits. Building will begin sooner than most of us could have hoped for."

"In some ways I'd like to be around to see the entire project completed," she noted with a wistful longing in her eyes. "It's going to be magnificent."

"It must be hard for you wondering what's going to happen from day to day," he returned, hearing the crackle of plastic as he loosened the cap. "Have you heard anything definite from the mission board?"

She shook her head. "On Monday they called to say the Congo was still unsecured for Americans and could remain so for several months. They still haven't heard from those in my village. They're the ones I'm concerned about."

"What made you decide on missions and going to the Congo?" The idea of missions intrigued Larry, and he had a deep respect for those who answered the call.

Becky smiled and fingered the lettering on her bottle. "It started a few years ago. Did you know I found Jesus only three years ago?"

He shook his head, surprised at the revelation. For an unknown reason he thought she grew up in a Christian home. Maybe her strong and hopeful faith led him to wrong assumptions.

"I met several students in college who were part of a Christian collegiate organization and decided to attend their meetings." She tilted her head and gave him an intent look. "Several weeks later I realized my previous views on God were all wrong. Being the best I could in life wasn't the ticket to God—Jesus was. I made a decision to follow Jesus in my life shortly after. Almost immediately I knew God wanted me to tell others about what He did for me—how He changed my life."

"That's when you decided to go overseas?"

"That's hard to describe." She took a sip of her water, seeming at ease speaking about this part of her life. "I guess I'd always been concerned about people from other countries who were in need. Now I knew how to help them not only physically, but also spiritually. My pastor encouraged me to talk with one of the missionary boards our church supports, and I suppose the rest is history."

"And the Congo?"

She laughed. "That was the hardest part. Every time they showed a presentation of a field in need of missionaries, I wanted to go. There were so many places in need and so few people willing to go. It was hard to make a decision. I wanted to go to all of the places. But what made my decision was the missionary couple in the next village who specifically asked for a single woman to work with a small Congolese women's group."

"And you liked the work?" Larry asked, leaning back on both elbows. He enjoyed watching Becky blossom.

"Oh, yes." Another smile spread across her face. "It took a lot of adjustment on my part, but God was able to use me in ways I'd never dreamed. The women were beginning to open up. Things were going well until I was awakened from sleep that terrible night and hustled out of the country." Her dark eyes regarded him solemnly. "It was awful!"

"I'm sure it was." He studied Becky intently for a moment. "And I'm sure you're worried about the people you left behind."

She nodded. "I'm praying for God to take care of them."

"It's a good thing you serve a God who has the power to make the impossible happen." He turned on one elbow. "Just like Kelly Enterprises donating the land. We were prepared for a long struggle haggling over the price—if we could even convince them to sell. And then—they donate the land. If that's not a miracle, I don't know what is!"

"God is amazing," she agreed, her face taking on the familiar glow he'd come to recognize.

"What does your family think of your missionary work?" he asked, watching her very closely.

Their gazes met for a timeless moment before tension slowly crept into her features and the glow dissolved like a water-drenched candle. "They weren't quite as supportive as I would have hoped." With that she put the water bottle down and brought herself up on her knees. "I suppose we should head back. You wanted to stop at the church, remember—and the secretary will be leaving for lunch soon."

He had no doubt in his mind: Becky's family was a source of anxiety. But why? Could she and her parents be estranged? It would be difficult to believe. Dreamers needed people and were generally close to their families. One thing was true; something was deeply wrong.

Becky was already gathering their tools when Larry finally stood, grabbed the tarp, and folded it into a nice, neat square. Silently they walked to his truck and loaded the shovels and cooler into the back.

"Do you want to drop in at the Dairy Barn for a hot dog after we finish at the church?" he asked, hoping to revive her previous mood.

"Okay," she acquiesced quickly as if their earlier discussion was long gone from her memory. "Are you going to try the special today?"

He turned in time to see the teasing glint in her eyes. "I told you before." He chuckled. "I don't do mystery specials. Living dangerously will kill you!"

"And police work doesn't qualify as dangerous living?" she challenged with amusement written across her delicate facial features.

"I have a firearm for protection on my job." He laughed. "What defense do I have against an unknown blob of ice cream?"

"It wouldn't do any good to shoot it."

"You've proved my point."

Both laughed as Larry pulled out of the parking lot. The trip to the church was a short one, and they quickly exited the truck. Larry opened the glass church door for her.

"Hello, you two," Tilly called out, shutting the office door behind her and coming toward them.

"Hi, Tilly," Becky returned. "What are you doing here? Searching for more volunteers to help plant flowers in the box out front?"

"Just droppin' off food for the pantry." Her eyes grew curious. "Heard some vandals went about diggin' holes in the fields of the camp property."

Larry nodded. "We just finished filling them in. Someone's probably trying out their metal detector looking for Civil War relics."

"Could be a specific Civil War relic they're lookin' for," Tilly replied mysteriously. She put her hands on her ample hips. "You know what I'm speakin' about, don't you?"

Becky looked as confused as he felt. "I'm not sure if I'm following you, Tilly."

"You don't remember the stories about the Union gold believed to still be buried on the island?" Tilly's mouth pulled to one side as she glanced between the two. "Legend has it that Union money was kept on the island, buried somewhere on Thunder Bay." She leaned forward. "They buried the money when some renegade Confederates were approachin' the island. They'd come to break out the Southern prisoners supposed to be held here. There's no way of knowin' if they knew about the secret Union treasury post, but the Yanks weren't takin' chances. They hid the money."

Larry rubbed his hand across the short crop of his hair. "I

do remember the story now, but it's never been proven to be factual. Most people discount it to great campfire tales."

"Plenty of island people are still believin' the story," she said. "It might be somethin' to consider. Whether the story is true or not, if someone believes—" Suddenly she gave them a wave. "I've got errands to run. Don't you kids work too hard now, ya hear."

Becky and Larry exchanged comical glances as Tilly breezed past them and out the door like a whirlwind.

"Come on," Larry said, walking to the office and opening the door. He let Becky walk through before closing it. He smiled at the secretary. "Good morning, Judi. Do you have the notarized forms for city council?"

"Of course," Judi responded, her eyes bright. "Signed and ready." She handed a white folder to him then picked up an envelope. "Something else arrived by courier for the camp this morning."

Larry scanned the official-looking envelope. "What's this?"

Judi only shrugged.

Becky looked over his shoulder. "There's no return address."

"Guess we'll just open it." He leaned over the counter. "Do you have an opener?" Judi reached into the desk drawer and produced what he needed. He slit the top and spread the sides open. "Looks like a check."

"A check?" Becky was stretching her neck to see.

Larry pulled the cashier's check and a short, typed letter from the envelope. He gave a low whistle. "The letter says the check is to be used for building materials at the camp. The donor wants to remain anonymous. What do you make of that?" He held it out for Becky to see.

Becky grew very still at his side. "Thirty thousand?"

"Thirty thousand!" He drew the check back and stared at the figure. What a wonderful show of God's support. Becky would no doubt add this miracle to her collection, reveling in the credence it gave to her dreams. He waved the check before her again. "Can you believe it?" He waited for her delighted squeal but instead watched her eyes grow wide and her face pale. His smile slipped. "What's the matter?"

She only shook her head before pushing past him and out the door. Judi's face mirrored his own surprise. He stuffed the check into the envelope then into his back pocket.

With a hurried stride he exited the office and out the side door. He stopped and scanned the parking lot for several seconds before glancing at his truck. A pair of white tennis shoes could be seen underneath the truck. It was time Becky and he talked, and there was no better time than the present.

eleven

Becky leaned her back against the cool sturdiness of Larry's truck, digging the toe of her sneaker into the gravel. Her thick mane of hair was unquestionably cleaning the fine layer of dirt from the driver's door, but she didn't care. Unbelievable! Michael or Father—or both—had managed what they thought to be thirty thousand reasons for her to return to California. Bribe money! Her chest hurt to visualize the check with the endless zeros mocking her very existence.

And she'd made a fool of herself in the church office, which all but required her to give an explanation. When would she learn to control her emotions? To match her mood, she heard the distant rumble of thunder and gazed up at the approaching dark clouds. Marvelous! Just marvelous!

The sound of approaching footsteps caused her to stiffen. Her heart gave an unpleasant lurch, and she looked to see Larry standing at the front edge of the truck. He said nothing for a moment then approached where she stood. Silently he leaned his back against the truck beside her.

"You'll be wanting an explanation, I suppose?" she murmured softly when the silence became unbearable.

"That would only seem logical," he answered briefly but firmly.

A warmth surged into her face. "It's rather difficult to explain."

"I suspected as much."

Becky closed her eyes and drew a deep breath. She felt his gaze upon her, and when she turned and opened her eyes, she met his intense stare. *Oh, this was hard.* "I know who sent the check!"

Surprise registered on his face. "You know the anonymous donor?"

Numbly she nodded. "It was Michael, the man you escorted to the hotel and met again last night on the campgrounds."

"Michael?" he repeated with a measure of skepticism, his eyebrows cocked in thought. "You believe Michael can afford such a large sum?"

"I have no doubt he has the resources to post such an amount and much more if necessary." She let her gaze drop to the police insignia of his worn black T-shirt; she knew what she would see if their eyes met, and she wasn't ready to face his contempt. The echo of "talking money" still haunted her thoughts.

"All right," she heard him say. "Let's suppose Michael did donate the money to the camp. It obviously upsets you to believe this to be true. Talk to me about what's going on."

Becky took a deep breath and looked up at him, noticing the power of his perceptive blue eyes. "I'm upset because it's bribe money!" Just saying the words caused her body to shudder.

"Bribe money?" His voice was acute, and she felt him straighten. "That's a serious allegation. What kind of bribe money do you believe Michael is offering?"

"He. . .and my parents want me to return to California."

Larry looked stunned. "And they're willing to part with thirty thousand dollars for you to go? That doesn't make sense, Becky. Why should they offer money to the camp in exchange for a visit home?" He tilted his head in deliberation. "Did you make some type of agreement with your friend Michael?"

Becky whirled to face him. "Absolutely not!"

"Then what?" he asked. "You said he was a 'childhood chum' if I remember right. Is there something else you need to clarify? Something else I need to know?"

His look and manner were too intense for her to pretend she didn't understand. Running her tongue over her suddenly dry lips, she slumped again alongside the truck's exterior. "We were college sweethearts," she began to explain. "I broke off the relationship when it became evident he wouldn't—or couldn't—share my new faith. My parents were devastated, of course, with my decision concerning Michael and then with entering the mission field. They carried on as if I'd joined a cult."

He seemed to give her explanation a frowning consideration then nodded. "Go on."

"They pretty much disowned me, both Michael and my parents," she continued, each word feeling like a hammer blow to her heart. "I hadn't spoken to either for nearly two years—until Michael wrote the letter and arrived unannounced two days ago. My mother suffered a stroke a few weeks ago, and he'd come to convince me to call my parents—or so I'd thought. His—or my father's—real intentions, I believe, were to have me go back home."

"Why would he assume it would take thirty thousand dollars for you to travel back to California?" His gaze was very still upon her, level.

Becky had to take a deep breath to curb the breathlessness she felt. "Michael and my parents are accustomed to gaining what they want with money. They're not used to being denied their wants." She paused long enough to gain a glimpse of Larry's reaction. When his expression remained unreadable, she continued. "They believe if the camp is given enough money you'll hire a new director to do my job, leaving me with nothing to do but come home."

"You're saying your parents and Michael are trying to manipulate you with money?"

The charged atmosphere crackled with tension. "Yes!"

"Answer me this," he asked, his warm hand suddenly grasping hers. "Are you positive the money is from Michael or your parents?"

"Reasonably sure." She pursed her lips. "He insinuated the offer last night, and the amount—well, it fits."

Larry's fingers released hers as he reached into his back

pocket and pulled out the envelope, holding it in front of him. The check slid out easily. "The cashier's check was obtained at a bank on the mainland two days ago. If we're to suppose the check is from your friend, it means he visited the bank the same day he came to the island." He paused. "And following that same analogy it means he would have anticipated making you the offer before talking with you." He shook his head. "Why go to the trouble of making out such a large check without knowing whether you'd object to traveling home? You hadn't seen or spoken with him in two years, right? As far as he knows, you might have wanted to go home."

"True."

"And," he continued, "he'd have to know you were working with the camp. The check is made out to the camp, not you. How would he have known?"

"True." His words were a cool breath of sanity she ought to welcome.

"Could it be the check might have an entirely different donor?"

A smidgen of doubt entered her mind, but she shook if off. "I just can't believe the check is a coincidence."

"Maybe it is; maybe it isn't." He slid the check back in the envelope. "Why don't you let me look into the matter and see what I can come up with?"

Larry moved to place the envelope back into his pocket, but Becky reached out, gripping his arm with all her strength. She felt his hard muscles move under her hands as he turned to her. "You won't—won't tell anyone about what I've told you, will you?" She let her hand drop. "I couldn't bear it if people knew. And if one person finds out, it will be all over the island in five minutes."

Something akin to uneasiness crossed his face, and a muscle twitched at the corner of his mouth. "I'll be particularly discreet."

She summoned a smile. "Thank you. I know this entire

situation must seem very peculiar to you. It's been extremely embarrassing to explain."

"I appreciate the fact you confided in me," he answered and then leaned close. "Is there anything else I should know? Anything which might be important?"

She hesitated, unsure of herself. "He did say one other thing."

"Go on."

"Before Michael left, he said he would be back." She paused. "With reinforcements."

He didn't respond at once but seemed to mull over her words. "Do you interpret his words to be meant as a threat?"

"I don't think so." She shook her head slowly. "It could mean a variety of things. Maybe he'll come back with a bigger offer of money. It could mean he's bringing my father to the island. It's hard to tell."

"It could be harmless," he offered, rubbing his thumb thoughtfully on the curve of his jaw. "Has he ever shown signs of being possessive or controlling in the past?"

"Possessive? Controlling?"

"Possessive and controlling as in constantly wanting to know where you are or who you're with," he explained. "Making you account for your time. Possessive and controlling as in discouraging your friendships with others and wanting you to spend all your time with him. Has he ever exhibited any of these signs?"

"No, never," she said, appalled at the thought. "He is strong-willed and likes to lead—you know, to take control of some decisions. But I've never felt threatened—annoyed, perhaps, but not threatened."

"You believe his remarks about reinforcements are harmless then?" he asked.

"I can't imagine what else they could be." A deep sigh escaped. "But I do believe he will be back, and if he gave this money"—she pointed to the envelope Larry still held—"he'll expect something in exchange."

"I can imagine this thought alone bothers you a great deal," he observed, his unwavering stare holding steady on her face. "As I said before, I'll make a few inquiries and see if we can clear up the matter."

"Discreetly!"

"Of course," he promised, tilting his head in the familiar way she found appealing. "I'll just need a small amount of information from you to help me begin."

"I'm sorry for being such a bother," she said with regret, letting her gaze drop. "I'm supposed to be helping you with the camp, not giving you more work."

"You don't have to explain further." He pushed himself away from the truck. "Come on," he directed, cupping her elbow to lead her around to the passenger door. Reluctantly she consented. "I promised you a Dairy Barn hot dog." He opened the door and waited until she settled into the seat. "I don't want you fretting about the check. I'll get to the bottom of it."

From his grim look Becky didn't hesitate for one moment to believe him. And although the thought of a hot dog squeezing past her constricted throat seemed impossible, she wasn't about to argue with the man who just climbed into the truck beside her. He was about to save her hide again.

⁂

Larry leaned back in the captain's chair waiting for the computer to process his request. "Is NCIC having trouble today?" he asked the lieutenant sorting reports at the next desk. "It's taking forever."

The lieutenant shrugged. "Everything's slow today. I ran a LEADS report earlier, and it took awhile."

Larry blew a puff of air from his cheeks. The National Crime Information Computer was becoming more and more vital to the department. They needed to invest in new computers with a faster connection.

A crack of lightning suddenly flashed light across his desk, and Larry glanced out the window as a deep roll of thunder vibrated the pane. Large droplets of rain were beginning to ping-pong across the outside ledge, and he glanced to the heavens. Dark clouds were moving quickly northward, but the promise of blue sky could be seen in the horizon. The rainstorm would pass quickly.

The sound of computer noise caused Larry to turn back from the window. Finally! The computer screen came alive, and he leaned forward to type in Michael Petit's name, date of birth, and last known address. Moving the mouse, he clicked several fields before sending the information off for analysis. The desk phone rang.

Larry scooped up the receiver. "Officer Newkirk."

"Got your message," the male caller responded. "What's up?"

Larry smiled and leaned back in the chair. The speaker's voice was unmistakable—fast, clipped and, as usual, to the point. "Yes, Robert. I'm fine—thanks for asking. And you?"

"All right, so I'm a little short on manners today," Robert returned with a gurgling smoker's laugh. He coughed. "Can't blame a guy for being on edge. The only time you call is when you need something. And why do I get the feeling you're going to cash in on the favor I owe you?"

"Because your feeling is right," Larry answered his old college friend. "I need your services."

"Ah," came the voice. "Personal or business?"

"Both."

"Spill it then." Larry could hear Robert ransacking his desk for a pen. "What can this PI do for you? Missing person? Bail jumper?"

"No." Larry tapped his finger on the check before him. "I need you to track down the owner of a cashier's check."

"Cashier's check?" Robert repeated. "That won't be easy, you know. What's the story?"

"I'd like to find the origin of an anonymous donor who has given money to the new church camp we're planning to build on the island," Larry answered.

"Yeah?" He hesitated. "You want to give the person a cigar or what?"

"Just need a name, that's all." Larry gave a brief account of the check. "Do you think finding the donor is possible? I know a cashier's check is hard to trace, especially if the person went to great lengths to remain anonymous."

"Yeah, but it's hard to move thirty grand and not be noticed," Robert pointed out.

"So you can do it?"

"If it can be done, I'm the one to do it." There was no arrogance in his voice, only confidence. "Is the check local?"

"First Community in Cleveland."

"That's good. Very good." More rustling of papers. "When do you need the information? Yesterday, I suppose."

"It wouldn't hurt to put some gas under the burner," Larry answered. "I'd appreciate anything you can do."

"I'm not saying my methods will be conventional, if you get what I mean."

"I don't want to know," Larry replied, knowing full well Robert's methods circumvented the law more often than not. He could use tools and gain information never available to law enforcement. But he was highly effective.

Robert only laughed and coughed again. "All right, buddy. Fax over a copy and let me check it out. As soon as I find something, I'll give you a jingle."

"And I need the inquiry to be discreet," Larry added.

Robert seemed to find this funny. "I'm the pillar of discretion," he said. "We'll be even after this matter is settled. You know that, right?"

"Right!"

"Is that all then?"

"One other thing."

"Yeah?"

"Give up the cigarettes, friend," Larry warned. "You're too young to be sounding like an old man with the croup. A guy of your talents needs to stick around for a long time."

"Sinus cold." Robert chuckled.

"Yes? And my badge is made of pure gold."

"Better keep it polished then. I'll give you a ring soon." The phone went dead.

Larry eased the chair back to an upright position and let the phone drop back into the cradle. Robert would put the matter to rest—one way or the other.

Becky's revelation had come as a total bolt out of the blue. What he expected her to say he didn't know; but it certainly wasn't a theory about the exchange of thirty thousand dollars for an unorthodox manipulation scheme. He wasn't sure which amazed him more: Michael offering the money, or the fact that Becky came from money—evidently lots of it. He prided himself in reading people well. He'd missed this one by a mile. He never figured her for a rich girl.

He plucked Robert's business card from the desk and scooped up the cashier's check. Making a copy, he went to the fax machine and punched in the mainland phone number. The second-long dial tone followed quickly with the high-pitched digital melody. Several seconds later he walked back to his desk with the copy and confirmation in hand.

Glancing at the computer screen, he noted the requested results beginning to formulate. He scrolled the information. Nothing! No outstanding warrants. No felony convictions. Not even an evil twin with the same name to prompt a follow-up lead. Larry folded his arms across his chest. He could call the Sacramento department and run a check for anything local—motor vehicle violations, littering, or even spitting on the sidewalk. Larry drew a deep breath. No, he'd wait to make the call after hearing from Robert.

"Hey, Newkirk!"

Larry turned to the lieutenant. "Yeah?"

"Line two. Sounds like a looker."

Waving off the remark, he punched the blinking red light

on the phone. "Officer Newkirk."

"Larry!" Becky's voice came across the line. "They've done it again. The holes are back, and there're twice as many."

"Where are you?" Larry asked, picking up his hat from the corner of the desk.

"At the camp."

"You're not alone, are you?" he asked with concern. "I told you not to go to the camp alone."

"Tilly's with me, and she's very upset," Becky said, her voice sounding troubled. "A nice gentleman who is touring the buildings is with us, too. He loaned me his cell phone to call you. What should we do?"

"Sit tight," he instructed, pulling the cruiser keys from the clip on his belt. "I'll be there in a few minutes." He replaced the phone and walked to the dispatch room. "Nora," he called to the uniformed woman sitting in front of the police computer. "Mark me code one at Thunder Bay."

twelve

"Larry's on his way." Becky told Tilly as she closed the cell phone and handed it back to the gray-haired man. "Thank you, sir."

The man acknowledged her thanks with a nod. "Hope you find out who's doing this," he said looking over the field.

"Foolish kids," Tilly responded, her hands on her hips. "That's what they are."

The man shrugged. "I'll let you women go on about your business. If you need the phone again, I'll be visiting the buildings."

"Thank you again," Becky answered with a warm smile and watched the man wander back to the opening in the trees. She turned to Tilly. "This is getting to be ridiculous. It'll take forever to plug all these holes."

"Enough to give a body indigestion," Tilly agreed, pressing her hand across her chest. She pulled a roll of antacids from her front dress pocket and unraveled the wrapper until two pink chewables dumped into her hand. She threw them in her mouth and grimaced. "Horrible tastin' things."

"What are we going to do, Tilly?" Becky asked, watching Tilly jam the roll back into her pocket. "Whoever did this had to be brazen to come in broad daylight. We just filled the south field holes this morning."

Tilly seemed to think over the problem. "It's gotta be kids skippin' school. They're after the treasure—I'll bet my loafers on it. They're thinkin' they'll strike it rich after listening to them ol' tales about Union gold. Some of these island kids don't use half the brains the good Lord gave them."

"Is there any truth to the story?" Becky asked as she turned to glance at the grove of trees in hopes of spotting Larry. "You'd said Union money was kept in the camp. Is it possible there *is* buried money?"

"The treasure *was* buried—that's for sure," Tilly agreed. "But it was dug up quick enough when the Confederates failed to make it ashore. There's nothing sayin' any was left behind."

Impatiently Becky patted the side of her leg and glanced at the trees once more. Still no sign of Larry. "Do you think it would help to have the newspaper do an article to debunk the tale? Maybe it would stop whoever's doing this."

"Mercy, no," Tilly answered. "You'd have every Tom, Dick, and Harry out here diggin' holes." She sighed. "Nope! We're gonna have to stake out the place to catch them rascals."

Immediately alarmed, Becky shook her head. "Absolutely not! Larry would have our hides. And besides it wouldn't be safe. Who knows what kind of person or persons are crazy enough to come out here and dig these holes? It might not be kids, but some lunatic."

"Never met a lunatic yet who didn't sober at the end of a twenty-two," Tilly pronounced with a grunt. "And Larry ain't got time to waste watching this place all the time."

Becky stared wide-eyed at Tilly, remembering the last time Tilly used her twenty-two rifle to pin down a thief at Piney Point. Lauren had just returned to the cabin when she noticed the open front door. The burglar bolted and ran toward Tilly's place with Larry in pursuit. Tilly jumped into the fray just in time to help Larry capture the man.

Becky had no doubts about Tilly's ability to fire a rifle with more accuracy than Miss Marple. And right now she wasn't about to give her the chance. Larry would have a royal cow. "You'd better keep the twenty-two under lock and key and let Larry handle whoever's doing this."

"We'll see," Tilly said noncommittally.

"You don't think—" Becky began then stopped. The idea taking form was too crazy.

"What?"

"It's nothing."

"How do you know it's nothin' if you don't say it?"

Becky blinked once, again passing the idea around in her head. "You don't think Mr. Edwards could be the one digging the holes, do you?"

Tilly let loose with a laugh that nearly shook the ground. "Van Edwards? Now why on earth would an old coot like him go breakin' his back diggin' holes?"

There was no offense on Tilly's face, but Becky wished she'd kept the question to herself. Of course Tilly would defend the man Becky suspected she might be sweet on. But there was no backpedaling now. Tilly would demand an answer. "It's just that he's been against settling the camp at Thunder Bay. What if he wanted to put the scare into the committee by digging these holes—you know, to stop any building?"

Tilly laid her hand on Becky's shoulder. "If you knew Van like I do, you'd be knowin' he wouldn't do that. He does everything legal-like, always above the table—never below. And he's good enough at the above-table approach not to need another approach."

How well Becky knew. And Tilly's answer did have some logic. Besides, the old man would probably keel over within minutes—still hanging onto the posthole digger. With a sigh she glanced back to the trees. Movement caught her eye.

"Help has arrived," Becky said with relief, watching a tall figure emerge through the opening in the trees. "Larry will know what to do."

"He's lookin' mighty fine in his uniform, don't you think?" Tilly's glance darted between Becky close by and Larry in the distance. "Mighty fine!"

"Behave yourself, Tilly!" Becky chided without rancor then smiled. Tilly was absolutely right. Larry did indeed look handsome in his uniform from the starched black pants to the ironed white shirt and dark tie. The shiny badge on the front of his police hat bounced shards of sunlight with each step. Pride swelled within. Larry might not be a dreamer, but he knew how to protect and preserve the dreams of others. He took his job seriously. That thought alone gave him a high rank in her book.

"Ladies," he greeted them as he came within speaking distance. In one hand he held stakes and in the other police tape. "More holes, huh?" His eyes scanned the field.

"Tilly wanted to see the grounds today, and this is what we found," Becky answered, sweeping her hand out toward the holes.

"Did either of you see anyone around?" he asked, looking from Becky to Tilly. "Anyone suspicious?"

Becky shook her head. "Only an elderly couple was touring the buildings. No one was here in the fields that I could see."

Larry walked over to the first hole and bent down to look at the ground. He let his fingers roam over various areas of the dirt. "They must have left right before you came. There are shoe prints in the mud here and here." He pointed to several places on the mound of wet dirt. "Whoever it was, they were here when we had the brief rain."

"They?" Becky asked, moving over to see the prints.

"Two sets of prints." Larry stood and moved over to another mound of dirt. "Maybe three."

Tilly followed the pair. "Kids?"

Larry looked up at the older woman. "Possibly teens." His attention went back to the mound of dirt. He traced a finger above one imprint then another. "I'd say a man's size eleven here and a possible ten there." His hand moved to the opposite side. "This print is much smaller. Possibly a woman's or girl's shoe."

"Can you tell what kind of tread or brand of shoe?" Becky asked, pulling her black hair back from her face as she leaned forward to see.

"The rain, however brief, also obliterated any fine details

on the shoes." Larry straightened. "Let me tape off the area. I'll have to come back in the morning to fill the holes." A concerned look crossed his face. "And I'd feel better if the two of you didn't come here alone." He pinned a look at Becky. "Call me if you want to see or show the property."

Heat rushed into her cheeks. "Of course!" In turn she gave Tilly a warning glance.

Tilly ignored the look and grunted.

"That means you, too," Larry returned, throwing a look Tilly's way. Becky couldn't help but wonder if he, too, wasn't thinking back on the burglary incident at Piney Point.

"We both understand," Becky announced, giving another cautioning glance to Tilly. When Larry turned his attention back to the field, she touched his arm. "Pick me up in the morning? It will go faster with two of us."

"Good idea!" Tilly chimed in with a satisfied smile before Larry could respond. "I'd help y'all, but you know this ol' hip of mine's been actin' up." She patted her ample hips as proof. "I'm sure Becky is well qualified enough to be a good helper and partner."

The look on Larry's face nearly made Becky choke. Tilly didn't mind being obvious, and the red creeping up Larry's neck didn't deter the older woman one bit.

Tilly fluttered a hand in the air. "We'll help you get the tape up, and then we'd better get goin'. I've got chores to do."

The three worked together in silence and had the stakes and tape in place in a short amount of time. They walked back to the parking lot.

"Same time tomorrow," he said to Becky. His look drifted to Tilly. "Remember what I said."

Tilly only smiled sweetly and waved him off before opening the door and plopping herself in the passenger seat of the car. Becky moved on past the car and followed Larry to his cruiser.

"I've made an interesting observation," she whispered, keeping her voice low and out of Tilly's hearing.

His brow lifted slightly. "What kind of observation?"

"Have you ever noticed Tilly's twang becomes more pronounced when she's scheming?"

"Is that so?" A warmth and gentleness had crept into his voice.

"It's true!" She watched the funny, indulgent smile light on his lips. "Sometimes she drops her *g* endings, and sometimes she doesn't. Listen closely and you'll see what I mean." She leaned nearer. "Her twang's thick right now, and that means she's scheming."

"I'll keep that in mind." Then his blue eyes darkened, and he gave her an intent look. "You're very perceptive. Just make sure you don't get caught up in any of her schemes. That dear woman has the entire island wrapped around her pinky and could convince the mayor himself to go along with one of her cockamamie ideas."

Becky smiled. "I promise." She had no desire to stake out Thunder Bay or see firsthand how good of a markswoman Tilly could be.

Larry opened the door to the cruiser and glanced over to her car. "Be careful, and make sure you get Tilly home before she has time to get herself in trouble."

Their eyes met in a flash of understanding, and Becky gave him a nod before walking to her car. Seating herself behind the wheel, she gave her companion a dubious look. "Comfortable?" she asked, knowing full well Tilly's hip complaint was much too convenient. "You're hip's not hurting with these seats?"

Tilly gave a hearty laugh. "In these small cars bad hips aren't the problem. The trouble with these bucket seats is that not everybody has the same size bucket."

Becky chuckled. "Oh, Tilly! What would this island do without you? I hope in thirty years I have your sense of humor and energy level."

"Old age isn't all it's cracked up to be," Tilly said with a wide, toothy smile. "Energy is all relative. The only thing I do with more frequency now is attend funerals and go to the bathroom."

Becky laughed again and started the car. "I'd better get you home before you have me in tears." In the rearview mirror she could see Larry sitting in his cruiser writing on a clipboard. His presence alone warmed her heart, making her feel safe in the midst of chaos.

"As long as they're happy tears, Becky." Tilly gave her a meaningful glance and popped two more antacids between her lips. "Always happy tears."

⁂

Becky flipped off the living room light switch, and the cabin plunged into darkness. For several moments she stared out the front window taking in the soft glow of the moon on the trees. Her heart felt content for the first time in weeks. Even the mysterious holes at Thunder Bay or thoughts of Michael and her parents didn't intrude. It came to her in a sudden blaze of understanding as she traced the windowpane with her finger. The camp's success was important to her because it was important to Larry. God had used Larry to fill much of the void left in her heart caused by the uncertainty of her future.

What if God chose not to send her back to the Congo? Wasn't He God enough to know and care for her Congolese friends in the best possible way? And if He chose to send her back, wouldn't He be God enough to fill the void she knew would exist from leaving her newfound rescuer? Yes, she could be content whatever God chose to do.

The faint sound of crunching gravel caused her attention to swivel to the road beyond. A small golf cart passed in the darkness, and Becky narrowed her eyes for a better look. If she didn't know better, the driver looked like none other than Tilly Storm.

She watched the small lights of the cart bob as it made a right turn onto Shore Lane and sped out of sight. Tilly didn't usually go out after dark, and it meant only one thing. Becky glanced at the clock. 11:30! If she hurried, she might catch Larry before he went off his shift. Carefully threading her way around the furniture, she found the lamp and switched it on before continuing past the dining room table to reach the wall phone. Using her finger as a guide, she scanned the small notepad with several handwritten phone numbers. Finding the right number, she dialed the police station.

"Sorry," the answering female dispatcher informed her. "Officer Newkirk has already left for the night. Would you like to speak with the midnight watch officer?"

"No, thank you," Becky politely declined and rang off.

Once again she picked up the phone and dialed from memory, this time to Larry's house. After several rings the answering machine with Larry's no-nonsense greeting came on. Disappointed, she let the phone rest back in its cradle. What should she do? Did she know if the driver was Tilly? The darkness didn't allow for good visual acuity.

Besides, what could she do anyway? Larry wasn't home, and he wasn't at the police station. Even if she left a message on his answering machine, she had no guarantee he would return home right away. After several minutes of deliberation she decided to wait and talk with Larry in the morning. It wouldn't hurt to pray for protection over the driver and the campgrounds for added insurance, though—just in case Tilly had a foolish idea of staking out Thunder Bay.

❧

"You didn't get a good look at the driver?" Larry asked the next morning as he rounded the turn into the parking lot of Thunder Bay.

"It was dark," Becky explained, her face solemn. "But it could have been Tilly."

He took a deep breath. "I wouldn't put it past her. She's tough as nails, Becky, and apt to take matters into her own hands, quite successfully the majority of the time. I'm more apt to be worried about the people she encounters, not her. They'll be the ones who will be sorry."

"I don't know," Becky said after a moment. "Maybe I should have left a message on your answering machine. It's just that you don't have much downtime between your police duties and the camp project. I didn't want to burden you with what I saw, especially if it turned out to be nothing. It might not have been Tilly."

He turned and gave her a smile. "Let me worry about my workload. You call any time you need me." He pulled the truck to a stop and put it in park. "I was probably on my way home from the station when you called. You can always leave a message."

"I appreciate knowing that."

He shut off the engine and turned to her. "Frankly I'm worried about you."

"Me!" There was shock in Becky's voice.

It was true. The camp project was taking on aspects he'd not bargained for, and Becky must surely be feeling the added stress of Mr. Edwards, suspicious donations, and the mysterious holes rapidly materializing across the camp property. And now, with good reason, she was worried about Tilly and her twenty-two rifle.

"A lot has been going on the last couple of days," he finally answered. "I'm afraid the work and circumstances are beyond what you might have expected for the job. I don't want you to feel the least bit responsible for solving all the problems or putting yourself in danger."

"Oh," said Becky, and she grew thoughtful. "Are you saying you don't think I can do the job?"

He saw a shadow cross her face and immediately scolded himself for failing to get his message across. He was much too concrete for his own good. "I'm not saying that at all," he replied gently. "I'm saying I don't want you fretting or losing sleep over the problems of the camp. You need to enjoy the island—maybe spend some time with Lauren and go shopping."

Becky frowned then. "I'm not fretting—I promise. I believe God will handle the problems." Her calm assurance almost challenged him to disagree. "I'm stronger than I look."

"I'm sure—"

She interrupted, her dark eyes widening. "God is my *total* strength."

His gut tightened. The fire in her eyes and assertive tone left him feeling strangely slighted. It was as if his own faithlessness was being bounced back to him by her very words. What was she trying to say? She didn't need anyone? She didn't need him? She evidently shared a close relationship with God that surpassed his own, for he did experience weakness and was known to fret over the details of life from time to time—well, maybe quite a few times. The thought caused him to draw back in his seat.

Had he read too much into her previous gestures and actions? Was this dreamer more self-sufficient than he'd first realized? If true, he would do well to prevent making a fool of himself. He'd had full intentions of asking her out for a nice, leisurely dinner at the Wharf that evening in hopes of exploring the possibility of knowing her better. Maybe it was time to squash the idea.

"Is something wrong?" She looked up with sudden gentleness in her face, her dark eyes concerned. "Have I said something to offend you?"

"Not at all," he said much more quietly.

"Sure?" Her eyes were a little apprehensive.

"Positive." He managed a smile then opened his door. "We'd better get those holes filled if we want to finish before noon."

"All right," Becky agreed slowly, opening her own door.

Puzzlement showed on her face, and Larry could have kicked himself for letting his heart become involved. Hadn't he warned himself the first time he laid eyes on her? How could one man be so good at giving advice and make a muddled mess of his own affairs?

thirteen

Becky walked out of the Balloon Boutique and into the early afternoon sunshine. The balmy air pushed her hair back as she lifted her face to the wind. Beautiful weather dominated the last week, and the island seemed to come alive with happy tourists ready for the weekend. She tucked the papers Flora signed into her purse. One more duty finished and ready for the groundbreaking ceremony. They would have only a few more days to prepare.

Quietly she walked the wharf and let her hand trail the heavily twined rope fencing. Her soul felt restless. Since the morning Larry and she worked together to fill those dreaded holes the week before, something changed. Larry changed!

Becky sighed and leaned over the ropes to watch a large family of ducks crowding near the pier in hopes of food. After a moment she reached into her pocket and deposited a coin into one of the numerous feeder machines lining the dock. Dozens of tan pellets poured into the mouth of the machine when she turned the crank. Cupping her hand under the opening, she lifted the lid and shoveled the food into her hand. The bobbing ducks grew noisy at the sound of the metal trap door opening, and Becky had to smile. Poor, pampered birds! She leaned over the rope again and tossed several pellets to the scurrying birds, watching as the pill-sized pieces dropped onto the surface of the water, dipping up and down with the light incoming waves. Dozens of openmouthed fish surfaced to the top for a chance at the floating food. When her supply finally diminished to nothing, the ducks continued to peck at the water, frequently glancing up at her.

"Sorry, guys," she called to them, stretching her hands out as evidence.

Then they caught sight of a young child several yards farther along the pier tossing handfuls of the alfalfa rations. The entire group of ducks paddled away without a backward glance.

With the momentary distraction gone her thoughts once again returned to Larry. How many times she'd gone over the scene of their last visit again and again, only to come up short. Everything had been fine until he suggested she might not be quite up to the job of camp director. Oh, he hadn't come right out and said it, but she knew what he'd meant. No doubt he was concerned about the vandalism and Michael's interfering donation. He was afraid the job was too much for her to handle. She tried her best to convince Larry she was up to the challenge—with God's help, of course, but the conversation fell apart shortly thereafter. What she didn't know was why.

Recalling Larry's earlier words about not falling for any of Tilly's schemes made her wonder if Larry hadn't been giving her fair warning to disregard Tilly's notions about any serious relationship between them. At the time she thought he'd meant Tilly's idea of staking out Thunder Bay. But in light of his swift and obvious withdrawal she couldn't be sure.

As a matter of fact, Larry hadn't spoken more than a few words to her all week, keeping any and all phone calls about camp business to a sterile minimum. He'd made no mention of his "inquiry" into the donated money either. Maybe he'd found something about Michael and her family. She didn't know how far or how deep Larry would probe into the money matter or what he might find. But if he discovered the truth about her family, it couldn't bode well for her. The thought caused her to shudder. What man—even a good man—wouldn't run when he discovered her dysfunctional past? Becky blew a lungful of air past her lips.

And worst of all? Her job as camp director had suddenly become duller than a last-period class on the mathematical principles of graphing parabolas and hyperbolas. Without the closeness she'd previously enjoyed with Larry, the new and exciting duties fell flat. What kind of godliness was that? She was supposed to be working for the Lord, not for the pleasure of Larry's company.

Tell my heart that, she moaned inside.

Now more than ever she desired to return to the mission field where at least her stimulating adventures weren't clouded by a man's presence. Everything seemed so complicated on the island! And her newfound contentment of waiting upon God for direction was slowly eroding. Larry's nearness and friendship had bolstered her faith and come to mean more to her than she'd realized. Without him, living and working on the island didn't cut it anymore. And she'd only been on the island for what—not even two months? Yet the distance she felt between them penetrated her very being with a deep and chilly coldness. Like an addiction, she'd come to rely on something or someone she never needed before.

God, what can I do to restore my relationship with Larry? He's a strong and godly man, and I like being around him. I like sharing my ideas and dreams with someone who really listens. Certainly You sent him to me—I mean, why else would he be around every time I've needed him? If I've done something to offend him, show me how to make it right. I don't want to lose his friendship. Yes, Lord, it does seem out of character for me, but it's true. I—Becky Merrill, the woman who has never needed a man—need Larry.

Becky leaned on the wooden support as she peered into her watery reflection. In all her years with Michael she never felt the same emotions Larry brought to her heart. She really, really liked—and missed—Larry. How could she have messed up the relationship before it even had time to begin? Somehow she had to fix what she'd damaged—if only she knew what she'd broken.

❧

Larry slowed his cruiser as he came upon Levitte's Landing. Tourists were beginning to trickle in for the weekend. Tonight and Saturday promised to be busy for the department, but he didn't mind. It was good to have the island up and running for the season.

He let his eyes roam over the shops and people before finally resting his gaze on a lone female standing on the pier. Without a moment's hesitation he knew the woman to be Becky. No doubt she had been visiting Flora at the Balloon Boutique to secure the balloons for next week's groundbreaking.

Gliding the cruiser to a stop near the entrance of shops, he straightened in his seat, never taking his gaze off her. Their strained relationship had an unnerving effect on him, and he found it plenty difficult to keep his distance from her. He felt drawn against his will. Yet she'd made it clear.

"Dispatch to one-ninety-four."

Larry stretched his mike closer and depressed the switch. "One-ninety-four—Shore Lane and Levitte's Landing."

"You have a mainland call. Would you like the call dispatched to your mobile?"

"That's affirm," Larry answered. "Send it through."

"Dispatching now, one-ninety-four," responded the female voice.

Larry's mobile phone rang, and he picked up the receiver. "Officer Newkirk."

"It's Robert." The raspy, no-nonsense voice was unmistakable. "I've got some information."

"Great! What do you have?"

"The thirty-grand check traces back to a Hague and Sullivant law firm in Cleveland," Robert began, clearing a loose gurgle from his throat. "I'd like to fax you a list of their clients to look at. Maybe you'll recognize a name." Larry could hear him drag on a cigarette. "Then give me a jingle, and I'll dig a little deeper if you find something."

Larry thought a moment. "Give me five minutes to reach the station and send the fax to the number I gave you earlier. I'll get the list from there."

"Will do!"

The line suddenly went silent. Larry took one last glance at the pier, but Becky was already gone. Probably a blessing for him, he reasoned. Looking at her only needled his gut with unpleasant sensations. Slowly he made his way back into traffic and to the station. He was anxious to see the list. He didn't care to know how or when Robert obtained a list of clients. All he knew was it was time to put the matter to rest.

A few minutes later Larry locked the door of his still-running cruiser and fingered the extra car keys dangling on his belt clip. More than one officer had locked themselves out of their cruisers, and he didn't plan to join their ranks. At one time officers didn't worry about leaving their running cruisers unlocked. But those days had passed.

He sprinted into the station and headed straight for the fax machine. Flipping through the tray of incoming faxes, he found the cover sheet and waited as two more sheets came through to be printed.

Rolling the papers into a nice cylinder, he walked to the corner cubicle to read them in private. Slowly he scanned the extensive list of corporations and individuals, drawing his brows together in concentration. Nothing looked familiar in the first column, and the second didn't look promising until his eyes stopped abruptly at a name near the bottom of the page. His mouth parted slightly in disbelief, and he withdrew a pen from his shirt pocket to circle the name. Interesting! More than interesting.

Several names later another prospect seemed to jump off the page. He circled it as well. An idea began to form as he looked at the mismatched pair, and he wondered at the ethical implications he might face if Robert continued the search. The results weren't what he expected—not at all. But what in life was? Gaining additional information about the names in question wouldn't evoke change, only enlighten a confusing situation.

Larry rubbed his chin in deliberation before resolutely picking up the phone to call Robert. He'd already come this far; he might as well finish the job. Whatever the result, let the chips fall where they may.

⋅❧

Becky threw off her covers. How could she sleep when her brain kept swimming with thoughts about her family and Larry? Her father had called that very evening in a tirade about the virtues, or lack thereof, of women who handled dirty shovels in manual labor. His response might have been delayed enough to catch her off guard, but he made up for it in fervor. She would have drowned soon enough if she let herself dwell on the scene many more times.

With resignation she walked across the room and pulled her robe off the door hook. She might as well get up. It was only midnight. For sure, sleep wouldn't come anytime soon, and it made little sense to force what wouldn't budge. Her bare feet padded down the hall and into the living room. Out of habit she stopped at the front window to stare at the peaceful scenery that usually calmed her frayed nerves. The task seemed impossible tonight.

She'd seen Larry in his cruiser at Levitte's Landing earlier in the day. He seemed busy with police work and hadn't noticed her on the pier. She made a quick exit before he spotted her. It was stupid really. Why did she have to avoid or hide from him? It was a nervous and infantile response to her emotions. Receiving the call from her father only added the icing—and a plump cherry—and a few caustic sprinkles—to her already ragged bravado.

The tall pines seemed to sway in response to her disposition. A sudden but dim pair of lights on the road caught her attention. The same golf cart she'd seen several days ago once again bounced down the road to Shore Lane. This time she was sure of the driver—Tilly Storm. It didn't take a rocket scientist to know where she was headed. There'd been no more disturbances at Thunder Bay since the day she and Larry filled the last set of holes, but Tilly had mentioned worrying about the weekend when police patrols would be occupied in town controlling the tourist crowds and drinking establishments.

Without hesitation she turned on a light and dialed the phone. Something troubled her more than usual about Tilly and her escapades. She had to contact Larry at the station. A woman picked up the phone.

"I'll dispatch you through to Officer Newkirk's mobile," she responded when Becky requested to speak with Larry. Becky waited, nervously twisting the curly phone cord around her finger.

"Officer Newkirk," Larry answered, his strong voice coming across the phone line.

Just hearing his voice caused her legs to quiver. "Larry, it's Becky. I'm glad I caught you. The dispatcher said you're pulling extra duty."

"Becky?" he repeated. "What's wrong?"

"Tilly left again in her golf cart a few minutes ago," she explained. "I'm almost sure she's headed for Thunder Bay. She thinks the vandals are going to strike again this weekend. Will you be able to check the camp property and see if she's there?"

"I'm on the other side of the island," he answered, "but I'll make my way over to the site. How long ago did you say she left?"

"Not more than five minutes."

"All right." She could hear him sigh. "Sit tight, and I'll call you once I see what's going on."

"Larry?"

"Yes!"

"Be careful!" A strong sense of disaster washed over her. "Something's not right, and I can feel it."

He was silent for several seconds. "I'll be careful."

The line disconnected, and Becky replaced the phone. She trotted to the bedroom and shed the robe and nightgown for a pair of jeans and a T-shirt. She wouldn't stick around the cabin waiting for a call. Not that she planned to interfere with Larry and his work, but she felt—no, she knew—God was telling her—Tilly needed her help.

God protect Tilly and her crazy attempt to save the camp from harm. Watch over Larry and keep him safe. He needs all the wisdom You can give him.

Locking the door behind her, Becky scampered down the deck stairs to the car. She only hoped her gut feeling was wrong. Nonetheless she felt God directing her course. How could she not follow?

When she came upon Thunder Bay she saw Larry's empty but running cruiser sitting in the parking lot with its high-beam headlights illuminating the grounds and buildings in the distance. She stopped her car several yards away, turned off the ignition, and cut the lights before slowly opening the door. An eerie quietness enveloped her when she stepped out from the car and silently scampered into the shadows across the parking lot. It was then she saw Tilly's cart partially hidden under a grove of trees. So Tilly was here! The thought gave her no comfort. She proceeded on, stopping several times to listen in the stillness for any telltale sound, only to hear the pounding of her own heart. Then a faint and remote sound seemed to skip lightly across the wind. Voices! She could hear voices.

She had to stop and think. If she continued to creep about in the shadows, Larry might mistake her for a criminal and jeopardize both of them. Not smart! If she exposed herself in the lighted parking lot, she might become a walking target. Also not smart. She'd sit tight as Larry previously suggested and wait. Something would happen soon enough even if it was Larry returning to his cruiser with nothing more than wet shoes from the dew.

In the darkness the swishing and thudding sound of some-one running grew steadily louder, and Becky backed deeper into the shadows. Two silhouetted figures dashed into the semilighted clearing then back into the wooded area until the sound of their steps faded into nothingness. The brief dim light, though, had been enough for her to make out the runners as the two teenagers who worked at Beckette's Souvenir Shop.

She stood glued to her spot. Were those two boys responsible for the holes? Why were they running? And where was Larry? Why hadn't he surfaced? Where was Tilly? The dilemma of what to do raged inside. Truly she was in a pickle. Either way danger for her or others might lurk.

More voices! Becky strained to hear the new voices and shook her head in frustration. She couldn't decipher where the voices were coming from, let alone who was talking. Cautiously she proceeded in the darkness until the voices grew louder.

"Ain't nothin' wrong with me," came the breathless voice she recognized as Tilly's. "Stop foolin' with me and go on and catch those kids."

"Not a chance!" This time it was Larry's voice.

"So you're keeping me against my will, are you?" Tilly retorted, her voice labored.

Becky finally drew close enough to see Larry standing over a crouched figure. Tilly? A glance around revealed no one else. What was Tilly doing hovering near the ground? The uneasy feeling returned full force. The only way she'd know or be able to help would be to make her presence known—without startling either.

She straightened. "Larry? It's Becky," she called. Her voice, very low, sounded strained and unfamiliar to her own ears.

"Yeah!"

Relieved, Becky relaxed her aching, clenched fists and moved from the shadows. A twig snapped as she stepped into the clearing. In one lightning motion Larry turned toward her, gun drawn, and she nearly sucked her lungs inside out.

"Police!" he shouted. "Stop right there, or I'll shoot!"

fourteen

Not one of Becky's six-hundred-plus muscles moved as she fixed her gaze on the black handgun entrenched in Larry's grasp. Time drew to a sure and paralyzing stop. When she heard slight movement from behind, her muscles constricted tighter still, and she feared they might burst from unabridged fear.

"Police!" the menacingly deep voice announced slow and hard from behind her in the dark. "You're covered in the front and the rear. Just put your hands up real nice and easy."

"It's me." She barely squeaked the words past her lips.

Larry's gun didn't budge. "Do as the man says!"

"Boys—it's Becky!" Tilly shouted, her words cut short with a groan of pain. "Put them guns down before you hurt her. Can't you see it's Becky?"

"Step out where I can see you," Larry demanded, ignoring Tilly, the black gun tilting ever so slightly. "Hands up and show yourself!"

"Nice and easy," warned the voice behind.

Becky forced her frozen limbs to obey, and she held both hands up and in view. "It's me, Becky," she said again, scarcely able to force enough air past her vocal cords to be heard. "Please put your guns down."

Slowly she watched Larry lower his gun, but he didn't relax. "What are you doing here?"

"I wanted to help," came her feeble response. She wondered if it sounded as dumb to him as it did to her at the moment. Had she misread God's cue? Even in the darkness she could see the stern and disapproving look firmly planted on Larry's face.

134

"Between the two of you, you're going to kill me with your help!" Larry snapped, slowly shoving his gun back in the holster. "It's all right, Kirk. She's clean." He pointed his finger in her direction. "Now move over here and keep out of the way," he ordered.

Becky immediately complied and moved toward Larry. Suddenly she caught full sight of Tilly kneeling on the ground and rushed to drop down at her side. "You're hurt! What's happened?" She tossed an anxious look at Larry and then back to Tilly.

"Nothin's wrong!" Tilly answered through clenched teeth. "It's overreaction, plain and simple. I'm fine as a fiddle."

Larry seemed exasperated as he hunkered down beside the older woman. He glanced at Becky. "Your supersleuth has bought herself a heart attack if my diagnosis is right." He felt for Tilly's wrist.

"Have not!" Tilly looked stubbornly at Larry, shaking her wrist loose.

"Chest pain, profuse sweating, and nausea. Need I say more?"

"Have you called the emergency squad?" Becky managed to ask Larry, placing her hand over her own thundering heart. The faint bellow of a siren seemed to answer.

"I almost had 'em," Tilly said, breathing with difficulty. "Those kids!"

"Stop talking, Tilly," Becky ordered. "You're only upsetting yourself, and that can't be good." Her own unsettled thoughts felt as clammy and cold as the wet grass penetrating the knees of her jeans.

The squad siren grew louder, and her gaze slid to Larry who looked up at the other officer. "Signal them in with your flashlight," Larry said. "They'll need to come to us. We'll never get her to the parking lot." Larry stood and reached for his walkie. "One-ninety-four to dispatch."

"Go ahead, one-ninety-four."

"The ten-twenty-four's on the scene. Please advise them to the back field location."

"Do you copy, medic two?" the dispatcher asked.

"Medic two copy and en route to back location."

Kirk moved forward and faced Larry. "You said two escaped north and one toward the lake?"

"Dropped their posthole digger where they stood when Tilly confronted them." In the moonlit darkness Becky could see Larry turn briefly to scowl at Tilly.

"I saw two teenage boys run into the woods," Becky interrupted with what she hoped to be helpful information. "It's the two who work at Beckette's."

"I know," Larry responded, clearly unimpressed. "It's the Johnson boys."

Kirk nodded with no impression of surprise. "What about the other one?"

Larry shook his head. "A girl, probably not more than fourteen, I'd say. She took off for the lake." He rested his hands on his hips. "I didn't recognize her, but once we round up the Johnson twins we'll find out who she is quick enough."

Kirk nodded in agreement then glanced behind him. "There they are!" He stepped out into the open field with his high-beam flashlight and began signaling the squad toward him with the steady advance and backward pitch of the light. Becky turned her face against bright headlights now bearing down on them through the field. The large box-unit truck bounced heavily across the uneven ground. When the fire department medic unit finally came to a rough and noisy stop, three men lighted from the truck, and Becky instinctively clutched Tilly's hand.

Give these men wisdom, Lord, to help Tilly in the best possible way.

Within seconds two of the medics had each grabbed an end of the heavy stretcher and unloaded it from the back of the truck. The third met Larry. He walked them over to Tilly, talking with the taller medic.

The tall one turned to Becky. "If you could let us in here, we'll take a look at this young lady."

Becky quickly moved back, but Tilly groused at him. "Young lady, my foot. I used to change your diapers, Milton Douglas Skaggs. Changed your mama's diapers, too!"

The young medic only laughed and after a cursory assessment directed the other two to bring the stretcher closer. With a flick of a lever they dropped the metal frame and cloth-covered mattress within inches of the ground. Seconds later and with quick precision they placed her on the stretcher, snapped it into high position, and rolled it over the short, coarse distance before hoisting her with great effort into the brightly lighted truck. Larry hovered by the opened back, hooking one hand over the top of the bright red door. Becky hung back and watched from behind as one medic took Tilly's vital signs and another attached white electrodes to her chest. Fear gripped her heart when the men's banter turned more serious.

"She needs to be med-flighted to Cleveland," the tall one told Larry. He stretched the EKG paper out like a scroll. "The sooner she gets treatment, the better."

"I ain't been sick a day in my life," Tilly protested, pulling her arm away from the dark-haired fireman attempting to tie a tourniquet on her upper arm. "I don't need one of them IV jobbers."

"Just settle down, Tilly," the tall medic gently told her. "Your condition is life-threatening, and unless you want to be pushing up daisies you'd better let us do our job."

Tilly grunted once more. "I should have left you in those diapers, Milton Douglas. Mighta taken the spunk outta you. Pushin' up daisies, my foot!"

But she didn't protest again, and a flurry of IV bags, tubing, drugs, oxygen, and beeping monitors took over the next several minutes.

"We have her stabilized," the tall one announced at last. "We're going to meet the chopper at the air strip. They'll airlift her to the Cleveland Heart Hospital." He backed out of the box and shut the doors of the truck with a decisive bang. He shrugged his broad shoulders at Larry. "Says she doesn't want anyone called. I'll leave that up to you, big guy."

Larry nodded, a grim look still set on his face. Becky felt drained and panicked inside. Larry wouldn't help her this time. He was too angry! The heat of his wrath might not be visible, but it would be a gross understatement to deny the fact that his fury was unquestionably burning a hole in her back at that very moment.

"I'm going to the mainland to be with Tilly," Becky finally said to Larry as the medic truck slowly made a U-turn and bumped out of sight.

"There's no ferry running this late," he told her, his voice still rigid. "It's well after one in the morning. You'll have to wait until the first ferry starts up at seven."

"At seven!" she repeated incredulously. She had to think. "What about the Express Boat Line?"

He looked as if he might not answer but finally shrugged and turned to Kirk. "Do you know how late the express is running tonight?"

"Probably did its last run at midnight," Kirk answered, his gaze fixing on Becky. "What?" He turned to Larry. "She wants to go to the hospital tonight?" When Larry nodded, he continued. "She won't catch a ferry out of here tonight, but I did see Tony Edwards at the Pizza Shack not more than an hour ago. He flew in today in his Cessna."

"Mr. Edwards's grandson?" Larry asked, seeming more than hesitant. "No, I don't like it. Even if he's willing to fly out tonight, he's been at the Shack. Too risky!"

Kirk shook his head. "Tony doesn't touch the stuff. Just like his granddaddy."

Tired of being ignored in the conversation, Becky finally spoke up. "Where can I find this Tony Edwards?"

Both men exchanged glances until Kirk spoke. "I suspect

he's still at the Shack. The worst he can do is turn you down."
He turned to Larry as if he had nothing more to say on the
matter. "I'm going to make a visit at the Johnson home. Are
you doing the honors for the paperwork?"

"Sure," Larry conceded. "Why not?" He looked at his
lighted watch. "I'm already pressing the clock for several hours
of overtime."

"The chief will be thrilled." He patted Larry on the back. "All
right then. I'm shoving off. Don't forget to get a few digitals
and maybe some prints on the posthole digger. You never know
what the prosecutor's going to want." With that he turned and
flicked a salute, leaving the two alone in the field.

A heavy silence hung between them as they faced one
another in the moonlight. And sure as rain, she knew the
explosion of thunder was about to unleash in a torrential
downpour upon her aching head.

"I could have shot you," Larry said in a low, controlled tone.

Becky nodded, tucking a few stray wisps of hair behind her
ear. "I'm sorry, Larry. It's just that I felt God was telling me
something wasn't right. I didn't mean to interfere. I'm really
sorry."

His eyes narrowed. "God does lead us in certain directions,
Becky, but I sincerely doubt He asked you to sneak out
here and scare me witless. I could have killed you. Do you
understand the ramifications of what that means? Do you
realize Kirk could have nailed you in the back? What possessed
you to jump out like that in the dark? Either of us could have
mistaken a shadow or a shirtsleeve for a weapon."

"I didn't *jump* out at you in the dark," she defended in a
strained calmness. "And I did call out to you. I thought you
said yeah, that it was okay."

"Well, I didn't hear you, and it wasn't okay! I was answering
Tilly, not you."

Stung to the core at his venomous tone, Becky stepped back,
holding at bay the misty tears threatening to come. "I don't

know what else to do, Larry, except to say I'm sorry again. It felt as if you and Tilly were in trouble—"

He stopped her midsentence. "I live in the real world, and so should you. You need to stick with what you know and can see, not feel and dream." He pointed his finger at her. "Real life has real consequences. Traipsing through the woods in the dark while I'm on a police call is serious business. What if I'd shot and killed you?"

How many times would he keep saying those horrible words? Undoubtedly she'd given him a terrible fright, not so unlike the one she'd received, but she hadn't intentionally tried to make his way difficult. Yet his words burned her like liquid fire. Did he purposely gain satisfaction by impaling her with as much pain as he could hurl? Another realization hurt even more—he'd just admitted his detestation of her ideas, her dreamerlike view of life. How could she have misjudged his openness so badly? Every time he'd patiently listened to her ramblings or praised her innovations, his recognition was nothing more than a farce. He'd never believed in her. Never! There was no mistaking his contempt.

Well, she thought with determination, she preferred to stick to her ideals even though someday, she was convinced, they would be blown sky-high. Maybe that day had finally arrived—for right now there didn't seem to be a scrap of any dream or hope flickering about within her bruised heart.

"I'm sorry. . . ." Her voice trailed off when she saw his unbending expression and slightly lifted chin. How many times could she keep saying she was sorry? She threw her hands out in frustration but found herself at a loss for words. There would be no convincing Larry of her intentions, not tonight or anytime soon—

Maybe never. He was too cool. Too in control. With a shake of her head she turned and walked to the break in the trees, not caring that her tennis shoes were soaked through with dew or that her bones ached with the rough jarring of her stride.

No sounds followed, and she knew Larry had no intention of pursuing her to ease his judgment or her excruciating pain.

Why didn't You leave me in the Congo, God? The physical danger there doesn't even compare with the emotional danger I'm facing on Bay Island. My faith is faltering, big time. Be with Tilly. . .and Larry and keep them safe. And keep me out of trouble! I know— that's a full-time job in itself!

&

Larry opened the cruiser door and threw his clipboard across the seat with more force than intended. Of all the asinine things for Becky to do! His hands still shook at the thought. Just reliving the moment, his gun pointing straight at her, his finger cocked and ready, made him want to explode with— what? Anger, terror, disbelief—possibly all three. Yet he was torn to shreds by the expression of hurt on her face. But how could he make her understand with mere words the gravity of what could have happened? There were no idioms or words in the English language to express how deeply the matter could have affected life itself. Becky and her touchy-feely dream world nearly brought disaster to them both.

Now she was off to see Tony Edwards. And he would fly her to Cleveland. All she'd have to do would be to bat those long black lashes of hers and the man would be putty. But right now he didn't care. He was too mad to care what she did. He was even too mad to pray. Maybe he was partly mad at himself for not recognizing her, but at that moment. . . . It would be a wonder if the two of them would be able to smooth out their differences enough to manage the camp business for the next several weeks. That could only spell trouble! Her bubbly imaginings would believe their opposite views could still work together, but he knew better. After all he was a realist, something Becky didn't understand. How could her virtues of unleashed faith lure him like a magnet, yet drive him crazy at the same time? He wouldn't have a bean left in his head if she continued to rattle him at every turn. Something had to be done! And soon!

❧

Becky took another tight-lipped sip of the terrible coffee as she watched the sun rise between the skyscrapers. The hospital's large plateglass windows needed to be washed, but the dirt didn't deter from the beauty of the yellow ball expanding against the orange and red backdrop. She turned to look at old Mr. Edwards slumped in the lobby chair next to her, his eyes closed in a semiconscious sleep. Lopsided glasses rested awkwardly across the bumpy bridge of his nose.

What a night it had been!

Tony Edwards agreed to fly her to Cleveland, but not before his grandfather insisted on climbing aboard the Cessna after hearing the news about Tilly. She'd never seen the elderly man move so fast. He was truly distraught over Tilly.

Tilly made it through the night, but she wasn't sure if the same could be said for the staff. Tilly fumed and fussed at the doctors and nurses with such fervor that Becky knew the brunt of her medical storm was past. Nothing, not even coronary disease, could beat Tilly when she set her mind to something.

Becky stood and stretched, feeling the soreness of her cramped muscles with every motion.

"How's Tilly?" Mr. Edwards asked groggily, straightening himself in the chair. He pushed his glasses up on his nose. "I didn't mean to fall asleep."

Becky gave him a small smile. "It's okay. Tilly's been resting for the past couple of hours. She's going to be fine."

"The doctors say so?" he questioned forcefully.

"Not in so many words," she answered. "I can tell though. She's going to be fine."

He flashed her a disbelieving look and stood to his feet. "I'll go see if there's anything new to know." He limped off slowly as if every joint had yet to wake up and join the human race.

Becky turned her attention back to the blossoming sunrise. Even Mr. Edwards couldn't muster enough faith to believe her. Just like Larry! Larry's accusing words still burned raw on her heart. Maybe she'd missed the boat somewhere. It was one thing when her unbelieving family chose to mock her faith and dreams, but coming from those who knew God—well, this was a new ball game, something she needed to think through.

"She's doing fine," Mr. Edwards announced, coming back around the corner and into the deserted lobby. "Nurse said the doc's going to do the heart catheterization this morning." A smile lit his face. "Tilly's in there giving them what for. She wants her breakfast."

Becky instinctively reached for his hand and gave it a gentle squeeze. "God's going to bring her through."

To her surprise he returned the grip. "I'm sure it means a lot to her that you came."

His words, the first kind words she'd ever heard from the man, were like a balm to her hurting soul. She only nodded and turned her eyes back to the window.

Tilly's heart would pull through this ordeal—of this she was confident. Too bad her own heart had no such guarantee. Her future was more uncertain than ever, and although Larry never physically fired his gun, he'd nailed her head-on with emotionally charged bullets. Now her wounded heart felt too riddled with gaping holes to hope for healing. She only hoped God would give her adequate faith and direction to keep going.

fifteen

Larry balanced the hot casserole dish, cornbread pan, fruit bowl, and dangling bag of cloverleaf rolls in one hand and rapped lightly on the door of Tilly's cottage with the other. Hastily he brought his hand back to steady the tall tower of provisions. The church secretary had asked him to drop off the concoction of foods when he'd stopped by the church earlier that morning. So here he was—Judi had called him an angel of mercy—delivering the homemade lunch to Tilly to aid in what they hoped would be a speedy recovery.

He had to smile. Angel of mercy! In his case the words might be synonymous with all-around good guy or church gopher. Whatever he was, his actions were quickly becoming popular with the women, young and old alike. He'd never enjoyed such notice. Once word circulated about his role in the apprehension of the three kids responsible for the mysterious holes at Thunder Bay, his reputation with the single women at church skyrocketed. He'd even managed to find time to take two of them out on dates this week and received one whopper of a kiss—right on the lips—from Mitzi Trammell again. And this time he didn't even have to unclog her bathroom sink to earn it. Not that he had much time to squander between the police overtime and camp duties, but the distraction of their company helped him cope. For while his status soared with the other church members, one person remained aloof and blasé.

"Hello, Larry!"

The sound of Becky's voice brought his attention front and center. There she stood on the other side of the screen door looking at him through the haze of wire mesh. The unreadable expression on her face caused him to tense.

"How are you, Becky?" he asked politely, shifting the weight of his packages ever so slightly. He should have known she might be helping Tilly on her first day back.

"I'm fine," she answered with generic civility, propping the door open for him. "And you?"

"Fine." He stepped past her, but not before he caught a whiff of her light and summery perfume scent. "Where would you like the food?"

"On the kitchen counter," she instructed, not bothering to move away from the door. "Right there is fine." She leaned lightly against the doorjamb, obviously finding no need to proffer assistance.

Larry struggled to let go of the plastic bag holding the rolls but managed to set all three dishes down without spilling. "How's Tilly?"

"I'm fit as a fiddle," Tilly broke in with a broad smile as she emerged through the back door and around the corner of the kitchen with Mr. Edwards in tow. She looked at the food and clucked her tongue. "Ain't no need for all this fuss. And look— Judi's even sent some of her famous fudge."

Larry walked over to her and planted a kiss on her cheek. "The ladies at the church are providing you with lunch and dinner over the next several days. So for once enjoy the pleasure of receiving instead of giving." His gaze pivoted to Van Edwards, and he extended his hand. "Mr. Edwards."

Mr. Edwards took his hand. "I never had a chance to thank you for taking such good care of Miss Tilly the night of her heart attack. You probably saved her life."

"Just doing my job!" he answered modestly and immediately wondered if he should mention Becky's role in the rescue. After all she was the one who alerted him, and without her call who knew what might have happened. He shot a glance Becky's way and doused the idea. Her impassive expression, however innocent, was colder than the frozen waters of Lake

Erie in January. Instead he said, "I'm just glad to see Tilly's up and around."

"Not that them doctors and their medical finaglin' aren't gonna kill me," said Tilly with a huff. Pulling out a kitchen chair, she plopped herself down. "Do this; do that. No salt, no fat—no taste. Lose weight—eat right, exercise, rest! Why don't they make up their minds?"

Mr. Edwards pushed his glasses up like an old schoolteacher and wagged his finger at her. "And you'll listen to the doctors. They know what's good for you." He patted her arm. "Now I'd better be going, but I'll be back again after dinner to walk with you. We'll only go as far as the birch trees this evening and maybe the big maple for tomorrow. We'll have your strength built up in no time."

"Don't leave on my account," Larry insisted. He couldn't be sure, but he thought a tinge of pink was beginning to show itself on Tilly's cheeks. "I've stopped only long enough to drop off the food, and then I'm off to run errands for the groundbreaking ceremony tomorrow morning."

"Groundbreakin's tomorrow?" Tilly exclaimed in surprise, standing straight to her feet. She ambled to the calendar hanging on the side of her refrigerator. "Today's the last day of April." She turned to Larry then Becky. "Neither of you has time to lollygag around with an old woman. Both of you shoo out of here!" She flicked her wrists at them. "Now go on. There's a lot of work needs done for that groundbreakin' ceremony. I won't have ya sloughin' off from the job on my account."

Larry smiled and held up his hand in defense. "I'm moving."

"Take her with you!" Tilly demanded, pointing an un-wavering finger at Becky. "There's nothin' for anyone to do now. I'm gonna eat and rest." She gave Becky a razor-sharp look. "Now y'all go on, and I'll call ya later. Van will be here later to look in on me."

Becky looked taken aback but gave Tilly a hug and promised

to check with her after dinner. All Larry could think about was the amount of slang Tilly was using and knew she was conniving to bring Becky and him back together. From the expression on Becky's face, she knew it, too.

Mr. Edwards stayed behind when Larry trailed Becky out the door. She stopped just short of the stone walkway.

"I'll be at Thunder Bay by nine tomorrow to make sure the balloons and refreshments are situated under the canopy," she said matter-of-factly. "Is there anything else you'll need?"

Larry rubbed his thumb over his forehead in thought. "All the groundbreaking tasks are on schedule, and no more help will be needed this afternoon." He paused and stared at her—hard. "But I do believe we have some unfinished business from last week which I'd like to discuss."

She raised her eyebrows at him and stared back. "I'm not sure what else you could say," she said softly. "You made yourself perfectly clear." Her chin tilted. "And for the record I don't find fault with you for speaking your mind the other night, but we do have to work together—at least for a little while—and I'd like to put any hard feelings aside during that time."

Her clinical tone matched what he'd encountered over the past week when they'd spoken on the phone. More disturbing was her ready agreement to anything he'd suggested. There was no debate. No fancy ideas or proposals of her own to interject. While he should be happy with her compliance, the change disturbed him. He knew he'd hurt her with his abrasive words, and though justified he had been too harsh. And now looking into her large dark eyes he could see the once glowing light of excitement in her eyes had been replaced with detached determination.

"Let me walk you back to Piney Point," he proposed, taking note of a fresh spark of resistance in her eyes. "I'm not going to sound off on you, if that's what you're thinking. I just want to talk with you—and to offer an apology."

"Why not?" she said with resignation after a long moment.

"It's not as if I have a choice." She turned and walked past him toward the wooded path.

"Wait a minute!" He stepped forward and caught her arm. When she stopped and looked up at him, he placed his hands lightly on her arms until he had her full attention. "I'm not your parents, and I'm not Michael. With me you'll always have a choice in what you want to do and whom you choose to be with."

"Is that so?" There was no anger in her statement, just skepticism. Without moving she let her gaze drop and linger on his hands, which were still gripping the striped cotton sleeves of her shirt. Slowly she drew her focus back and met his blue gaze with challenging force.

"Sorry!" Larry abruptly released her.

"All right," she said, gesturing with her hand toward the path. "You have my attention—let's talk."

Larry fell in step with her. "I behaved rudely the other night, and I want to apologize for my harshness. What I had to say could have been said with much more grace and tact, and I know your feelings were deeply hurt by my insensitive handling of the situation. I reacted off the cuff and without excuse."

She turned and looked at him. "Yes, you could have been gentler, but you did speak the truth. I shouldn't have come to the field that night when you told me to stay. I put you in a bad situation, and for that I'm sorry."

"It's hard to convey the adrenaline push and life-preserving fear that comes over a police officer when that gun is pulled, cocked, and ready for action." Just talking about the episode sliced his gut like a fresh wound. "I've only had to draw my gun three times, and unless you've been there and done that, it's impossible to understand the depth of emotion behind that very act." He inhaled deeply. "It is unthinkable to contemplate, Becky, what could have happened that night. If Kirk or I would have. . ." His voice trailed off.

Becky shook her head. "You don't have to make any excuses for your anger, Larry. I accept full responsibility." Her delicate shoulders lifted lightly. "I suppose in a way it was good for you to lay out what you thought."

"No, it wasn't!" he protested.

She moved forward, reaching out to push back a branch extending into the path. "You said things that needed to be said, and you were right! I need to stop envisioning myself as someone who can save the world and everyone in it with my lofty ideals. I need to start living in the real world."

"Whoa!" He touched the sleeve of her shirt again, and she impatiently turned and stopped. "Under no circumstances should you try to dismantle who you are. I never, ever meant to give that impression." He took a deep breath and sent a wordless prayer for wisdom. "You are a lovely woman inside and out. What I tried, ever so badly, to say the other night was that you need to use discernment with the gifts God has given you. God has given you insight into people—how they think, how they function, and what they need. He gave you insight the other night that Tilly was in trouble, but that didn't mean He wanted you personally to rescue her."

"But—"

Larry shushed her. "God doesn't expect you to go it alone. That night He gave you another person to handle the rescuing." He tapped his finger to his chest. "That someone was me. You need to accept not only His gifts, but His provisions, as well."

"Why is it so complicated? All I want is to do what God wants me to do!"

"Then do it!"

"That's the problem. I don't know what I'm supposed to be doing." She began walking the trail again, her words still strangely distant and uninvolved. "Last year I thought my life's work would be spent in the Congo. Now it doesn't look the least bit promising that I'll be able to return. And this camp project? I'm not sure I'm cut out for it. Mr. Edwards might have been right from the start."

"In what way?" he asked, continuing to feel unsettled with her demeanor. Her words were far-reaching but uncharacteristically dispassionate.

"I'm the stick between the spokes that makes the wheels stop rolling."

"Explain to me what that means."

"It means that what I have to offer you and the camp is more detrimental than helpful."

"I'm not sure how you came to that conclusion, but it couldn't be further from the truth." Larry had to think a moment. "Sure—there are times when certain ideas and plans won't pan out. But just because some of your ideas fail, it doesn't mean the entire program won't work."

Becky shrugged as she continued walking and didn't appear ready to answer. Larry tried again.

"For instance, take your idea about building the cabins near the lake. Jason has worked out a blueprint to make at least one of those cabins work." As the path widened out near Piney Point, Larry pulled up beside her. "Now me—I'd already written off the possibility of building on that portion of the parcel. Being the concrete-type person I am, the obstacle didn't seem to be worth the effort. Now you—you had the dream, and without your persistence the idea wouldn't have become a reality."

At this, Becky halted and swiveled toward him. "And without me it wouldn't be costing the camp another seven thousand dollars to make it work," she said in frustration. "And the camp wouldn't need a thirty-thousand-dollar check from Michael."

"Ah!" Sudden understanding lit upon him. "If that's still bothering you, you can stop worrying about the money," he assured her. "Neither Michael nor your father sent that check!"

This seemed to catch her attention. "How can you be sure?"

"I can't tell you right now. You'll just have to trust me that it's true."

Her lips pursed and tilted to one side in wariness. "If the check didn't come from Michael or my father, then who did donate the thirty thousand?"

"I can't tell you that either."

Something akin to a ladylike snort escaped her lips. "Top secret?"

"In a way—yes." Larry expected news from Robert any day to confirm or disprove who he believed the donor to be. Even then he wasn't sure whether the information would be of a sharing nature. "I promised to look into the matter, and I did. I didn't find anything to suggest that your friend Michael might be a physical threat or that he was the author of the generous donation. Beyond that, you'll have to trust me with the rest until I have more information."

"More information?" she repeated.

"Perhaps!"

He could tell Becky wasn't satisfied, but she let the matter drop. "Let's just get through the groundbreaking ceremony tomorrow. I'm having a hard time thinking beyond refreshments and balloons at the moment. Do you think we can work together—at least for the interim until I decide what I'm going to do?"

"You're thinking of resigning the directorship?"

"That's a possibility."

"What would you do?"

"I'm not sure." The question seemed to make her nervous, and she began walking the leaf-covered trail again.

"Fair enough!" With great effort he concealed his dismay and fell in step beside her. "I don't see why we can't make this work. The incident the other night was just that—an incident. We can work together."

"Thank you for understanding."

He understood, but did *she* understand? How could he make her understand what he couldn't comprehend? The thought of her leaving the project and possibly the island sent an odd alarm through his core. In the past two months he'd grown to like her quirky ideas and dreams even if they weren't always feasible. *Tell the truth, Newkirk!* he demanded of himself. He'd grown to like her. Not that he would have admitted it the night she nearly scared him out of his six-foot-two skin. In the clear light of day, however, he couldn't deny the attraction between them.

Piney Point came into view, and once again Larry marveled at the picturesque scene the cabin made against the tall pines.

"Wonder whose car that is?" he heard Becky ask.

Larry caught sight of the full-size burgundy sedan parked just below the property on the narrow road. It wasn't an islander car. He knew every vehicle owned by the locals. As they rounded the side of the cabin to the front deck, he heard Becky's quick intake of air.

"Michael?"

The lone figure standing up top suddenly turned at the sound of her voice. The unmistakable dark curly hair and proud face left little doubt that the man was Michael. But it was the appearance of a man and woman walking near the deck's edge that seemed to make Becky stop dead in her tracks. He watched as every scrap of color left her face.

"Your parents, I presume?" he asked dryly.

Numbly she nodded. "When Michael said he was bringing reinforcements, he should have told me his weapons of mass destruction came in tandem."

sixteen

"The missing daughter returneth," Michael called down to Becky with a swaggering smile, leaning over the deck as her parents gathered to the edge beside him.

Becky looked up and shielded her eyes from the sun with her hand. "Michael!" she acknowledged softly before letting her gaze rest on the couple. "Hello, Daddy. . .Mother." What a marvelous and wretched development this was. She turned to Larry with a grimace. "You might as well meet the clan."

She led the way to the front and agonizingly drew herself up the wooden steps to the landing. Once at the top she attempted to take in a calming lungful of air. Even the feel of Larry's reassuring hand on her arm did little to quiet her jittery nerves.

Her father was the first to accost them. "So you must be the police officer friend Michael has told me about." He gave a piercing look Larry's way. "You should have instructed this daughter of mine to invest in a decent lock for this place. A single girl shouldn't be protected with such a flimsy piece of junk."

Becky jerked her gaze to the cabin and felt her hands shake. "How did that door get open?" she demanded, feeling the blood pump into her face.

Michael lifted a credit card between two fingers. "Piece of cake."

Had the man no shame? And right in front of an island policeman. "In civilized circles we call that breaking and entering," she retorted.

"Stop being melodramatic," her father chided, pressing down his wind-ruffled patch of combed-over hair. "Michael's only giving you a visual illustration to make a point. The lock's a flimsy excuse for any security." His eyes once again darted to Larry. "Wouldn't you agree with that?"

Becky felt Larry shift beside her, but her petite mother stepped forward before Larry could respond.

"Do stop all the harping," her mother droned, stroking her father's arm. "I haven't come all these miles to argue. I want to take a look at my little girl." She gave Becky a delicate and stiff hug.

"Mother, you should have called," Becky returned, clenching her teeth with the seething anger building within. Ambushed! She'd been purposely ambushed. Even her sweet-smiling mother was in it for all she was worth. Why couldn't she have a normal family where reunions were a happy affair?

"We decided to come at the last minute," Michael threw out with a shrug. "Your parents wanted to be here for the groundbreaking ceremony you've talked so much about. We've come to support your work!"

Liar! Liar! Pants on fire! she wanted to retort. But kids' games wouldn't work on this crew. No, the three were a formidable force. As if sensing her distress, she felt Larry move closer, his hand now resting on the small of her back.

"A proper introduction is in order, don't you think, Becky?" she heard Larry ask in a debutante tone. "Maybe you could do the honors."

She almost smiled at the scowl blossoming on her father's face. His lack of manners had been glaringly exposed. "Certainly," she answered. "Larry Newkirk, I'd like you to meet my father and mother, James and Lolita Merrill." She waited as Larry extended his hand to both. "And you've already met Michael."

"Yes, it's a pleasure." Larry shook Michael's hand. "I'm glad you found the island worth a second visit."

Michael eyed him shrewdly. "Becky makes it worth it, you understand—and I'm sure you won't mind if we kidnap her for the rest of the day, will you?"

"Of course he won't mind!" her father boomed. "We're her

family after all. Mr. Newkirk can understand that." He gave Larry a barbed look before nailing Becky with one. "Especially since our daughter hasn't seen fit to visit us."

Becky nearly popped a cork at their audacity. Something had to be done—and quick. Suddenly she pulled her arm through Larry's and leaned against his shoulder.

"I really hate to disappoint all of you," she began with a smoothness and repentant flare she didn't think possible. "But Larry and I have an engagement tonight which can't be broken— a working sort of deal. I really wish you would have called, and we might have been able to include you in the reservations."

"It is a shame," Larry added without missing a beat, and she could have kissed him. He looked at his watch. "And we're running behind!" She intercepted his look. "We might have enough time to see your parents and Michael to the hotel."

Lolita sputtered. "But, dear, I thought we could stay here with you."

"Here?" Becky feigned surprise, gaining strength from Larry's strong presence. "That's impossible, Mother. There's no room prepared." She leaned forward and lowered her voice. "You know my former employer and his wife are letting me stay here rent-free, and I couldn't impose on their generosity by asking them to fix up another room."

"I never!" her mother exclaimed.

Maybe it's time you did! She turned to Larry. "Let me go in and grab my bag. We'll show them to the hotel." She suddenly stopped and turned to Michael. "You did make reservations? It's May Day weekend, and there won't be a hotel room left on the island."

Michael glowered. "Yes, but I reserved only one room— for me."

"Oh, dear," Becky went on. She looked at her parents. "I hope you won't mind sharing a room with Michael."

"Sharing a room?" her father exploded. "No, that won't do!"

"There might be some rooms left on the mainland," Becky

offered. "Would you like me to call around?"

Her father worked his jaw back and forth, and Becky felt sure he was ready to spit nails. Although she believed in God's command to honor parents, she knew God didn't expect her to lie like a lifeless doormat for their verbal abuse and power plays. Their last phone call still needled her. Her father asserted that God had proved him right. God never intended for her to go overseas and kicked her out of the Congo to get it through her thick and stubborn skull.

And from the looks of it she was about to receive another share of his venomous judgments. Sweetly she turned to Larry. "Would you mind fetching my purse from the cabin? I'd like to have a word alone with my parents." She let her gaze drift to Michael. "Michael, would you go with Larry and help him look?"

Michael looked defiant.

Larry gave her a troubled glance. "Are you sure?"

She nodded and watched with gratitude as Larry approached Michael. Whatever he said to Michael made him compliant. As soon as the two disappeared into the cabin, Becky turned to her parents.

"Now, you look here—" her father began.

"No! It's your turn to listen." Becky kept her voice low, but she felt a deep force and God-given power behind the words that made her father quiet. "I've listened patiently to your words for some time, and now it's time for you to listen to me." She bent her head slightly. "I want to love you and enjoy the relationship a daughter should have with her daddy, but I find it impossible to do so. I've been praying for guidance on how to approach the issue, and I guess my only solution is to deal with the problem head-on." Coolly she tucked several strands of loose hair behind her ears. "You might think it's helpful to offer your opinions, and I'm not averse to accepting constructive guidance; but I can no longer tolerate the verbal abuse."

"What rubbish is this?" her father snapped, and his forehead vein began to budge.

"Be quiet and let her finish!" Lolita demanded, much to Becky's surprise.

She took the opportunity to forge ahead. "I'm offering us a chance to be like a real family," Becky continued. "But we'll need to have ground rules for this to work. I can't function under the stress of being judged, sentenced, and strung up. I want to be treated like a human being and respected as a daughter. In return I'll love you as a daughter should." A thick lump formed in her throat. "If you feel that you're unable to treat me with respect, then—then we'll have to part ways."

"That's the most supercilious—" Her father seemed at a loss for words.

"Now, James," Lolita said, throwing a worried glance Becky's way. "Maybe you should listen—"

"No," he barked. "I won't listen." He stepped toward Becky. "You always were the difficult one. Why couldn't you be like your brother? If you'd listened to me instead of being so mule-headed, you'd be successful—instead of living on handouts." He seemed ready to continue his tirade, but she cut him off.

"You need to make a choice, Daddy," Becky demanded, standing firm and straight even though her muscles felt like jelly, ready to collapse in a puddle. "I've tried letting your remarks pass over me. I've even tried tuning you out." She spread both hands before them. "I've tried talking calmly and respectfully with you. I've tried showing you what the love of God has done for me and could do for you." A deep sigh escaped. "You cannot judge and tell me what God wants or doesn't want for my life. You don't even know Him!"

He sneered. "So now our turncoat daughter is too good for her family? Is that it?"

Becky held her ground. "If you cannot continue this conversation without insults, I must ask you to leave."

As if she'd physically slapped him, he stumbled back in a rage. "Then so be it!" He turned toward the door of the cabin. "Michael, come out here!" With a malicious glare he turned back to her. "I'll disinherit you!"

"Then so be it," she repeated. His threat might intimidate her brother, but it proved he knew nothing of her heart. She didn't want his money, only his love and acceptance—something he appeared incapable of giving.

When Michael appeared at the door, her father brusquely motioned him out. "We're leaving." He threw a spiteful look at Becky. "You've been a great disappointment to your mother and me." With that he thundered down the steps and toward the car.

Lolita looked lost and gestured helplessly to Becky. "Your father's only trying to help you."

Becky sadly shook her head. "Love doesn't behave that way, Mother—pride does. And I'm sorry he's chosen pride over me."

Lolita gripped Becky's arm in desperation. "You'll give him a heart attack!"

"You can't lay that at my door," Becky insisted with confidence. "He's doing this to himself. I will no longer take the blame for his behavior or any other physical malady either of you might endure."

Michael came closer cautiously and glanced over the railing as her father swung open the car door and hurled himself in. "Whatever did you say to him?"

Becky turned to Michael. "The same thing I'm going to say to you. I want to be treated with respect and will no longer tolerate contrived impositions, bribes, coercion, or guilt trips." She took his hand and looked him in the eye. "God does love you, and I will continue to pray that you'll one day discover Him. And for what it's worth—I'll miss you. We did have something special."

"You're sounding very final."

Becky nodded. "I think when you talk with Daddy, you'll find it's very final." She gave him a sad smile. "And I know you well enough to know you won't cross him." She turned and looked at her mother. "I'll miss you, too. If you and Daddy change your mind, you know my number."

Michael slowly shook his head and gave her a now-you've-done-it look before taking hold of her mother's arm. "Come on."

Without a word they reluctantly proceeded to the landing and down the steps. Becky watched as Michael helped her mother into the car then took command of the wheel before driving the three out of sight. She didn't move until the soft sound of footsteps from behind caused her to turn. Larry stood not more than four feet away.

She tossed her hands out in a careless gesture. "I'm sorry you had to witness that wretched part of my life." She could feel her brave façade begin to crumble. "But there it is! The good, the bad, and especially the ugly."

He shook his head. "I had no idea."

"Most people don't." What else could she say? There was nothing left. The scene had said it all. She'd done the impossible and stood up for what was right! And the event had played out exactly as she'd imagined—not hoped—but imagined.

"I'm sorry your family put you through that," Larry said, stepping close to open his arms in invitation. "I never knew."

She let herself drop against his chest and be enveloped in the warmth of his embrace. The steady rhythm of his heartbeat gave a numbing comfort. What must Larry think? He'd seen the raw and exposed baggage she called life. In truth she was relieved to settle the matter with her parents even if it went badly. What she hated was the fact Larry had been witness. What man would want emotionally damaged goods in need of repair? And how could God be pleased with her when her biggest concern at the moment wasn't her parents at all, but Larry's reaction to the whole thing? She was a failure as a missionary, unmanageable as a dreamer, and orphaned by necessity. It could only mean the third strike in the bottom of the ninth. But there would be no tears. She couldn't—wouldn't—allow it!

Finally she pulled back. Finding the courage to look at his face, she was surprised to see his eyes were damp. What a pathetic creature he must think she was. She turned away, but his grip tightened around her.

"I'm sorry you've had to endure such abuse from the ones who are supposed to love you the most," he murmured into her hair. "It makes me feel that much more like a heel for treating you so terribly the other night."

"It's not your fault." She drew away. "I regret you had to be here when this happened." She gazed up at him. "I gave my parents an ultimatum, and I'll have to live with the results."

"You did what was right and what you had to do in order to survive," he said.

She gave an unhappy laugh. "Am I heartless to feel such relief from booting my parents off the property? I mean, it's like a heavy weight has lifted from my chest."

"Not heartless," he insisted. "Just human!"

"And alone!"

Larry tipped her chin with his fingers. "You won't be alone as long as I'm around." He smiled down at her. "Why don't you go inside and freshen up? Then we'll go out on this big engagement we have."

"I'm sure you don't feel like going out any more than I do," she answered with a small smile.

"Maybe so," he laughed. "But we've already announced our plans, and I for one don't want to be accused of being a fraud."

She shook her head. "I don't know."

"You don't care that God will hold me accountable for aiding and abetting your failure to keep a date?"

"Well, when you put it that way—" she answered. Not that she felt like going anywhere but to the couch where she could lick her wounds.

"Trust me," he whispered. "When the horse throws you, it's time to get right up and try again."

Becky nodded and walked into the cabin. Why was life so complicated, and when was God planning to let the pieces of her life fall back into place?

seventeen

Larry stroked the light stubble of his beard and pulled his electric razor from the bathroom cabinet. The razor slid over his skin in even strokes. Twice he stopped to feel for rough spots. Today was the groundbreaking ceremony, and he wanted to look good.

He'd also requested the afternoon off his scheduled shift. It was time to cash in on the mounting units of comp time he'd earned. Certainly it was inconvenient to the department with the May Day celebration, but he had more important plans— Becky. She just didn't know it yet.

Larry paused to check his reflection in the mirror then reapplied the razor to a missed spot. When the phone rang he did another cursory look and feel of his chin. Satisfied, he replaced the razor in the cabinet and trotted off to the living room phone.

"Got your information, Newkirk," Robert announced as soon as he lifted the phone.

Larry laughed. "You're awfully cheery for six-thirty in the morning."

"Yeah, I know it's early, but I did try calling the office." He coughed. "Thought you wouldn't want to wait until your next duty day."

"What do you have?"

"I might add the information wasn't easy to obtain," Robert continued. "This guy's a real Houdini when it comes to hiding money."

"The man and the corporation are one and the same, aren't they?" Larry said.

"Yep." Robert wheezed and cleared his throat. "Kelly Enterprises is owned by Van Franklin Edwards and the distributor of your anonymous sum of thirty grand."

"I knew it!"

"And we're even, right?"

"Even!"

"Anything else you want will cost you big time," Robert asserted with a quick and watery laugh. "As usual it's always a pleasure doing business with you."

Larry smiled. "You did good work! Come visit the island anytime, and I'll treat you to a real seafood dinner."

"I might take you up on it as long as it's a real restaurant, not some pressed-fish and patty place. As I remember, you were always a big cheapskate."

"All lies!" Larry laughed.

"Yeah, well—we'll see when I really do show up and order the biggest lobster on the menu."

"It'll be my pleasure."

"Whatever!" He coughed again. "I'll let you know."

The phone line went dead, and Larry replaced the receiver. So Mr. Edwards wasn't the destitute Dairy Barn employee everyone took him for. He cashiered and bussed tables in an establishment he probably owned. The news caused him to laugh aloud. The old man had everyone fooled.

And they'd stay fooled!

He had no intention of sharing the secret with anyone, not even Becky. No wonder Mr. Edwards caused such a ruckus at the camp committee meetings. He was practically funding the entire project—as well as other church projects, no doubt. Once convinced the camp project was financially solid and worthy in cause, he'd donated the Thunder Bay property and the anonymous gift of money. The news blew his mind. He chuckled again as he walked to the bedroom.

Larry tucked in his shirt and went to the armoire in search of a thin black belt. He threaded the belt through the loops of his dress pants. Snapping the belt into place, he ran a hand over his cropped and bristly hair. Next came the tie and suit coat. Today would be a good day. Things were beginning to fall into place.

&

Becky tied the last two balloons on the end of the table and stepped back to assess her work. Twice she moved the small plates and napkins. Twisting her watch into view she looked at the time. Nine o'clock. Not only had she arrived early, but also the work took less time than anticipated. She wanted the ceremony to be flawless. It might be her last chance to work on the camp project.

She opened the lid on one of the coolers and checked the platters of foil-covered finger sandwiches for the third time. The nervous jitters always made her compulsive. It wasn't as if the sandwiches were going to disappear. There was nothing to worry about. Even the mysterious holes thriller had been solved.

It was all so ridiculous anyway. The Johnson boys were charged with a first-degree misdemeanor, and the neighbor girl who was not more than eleven was doing community service. Tilly hadn't been far from the truth that the youths were seeking treasures. Their distorted version of the Union money tale, however, had the boys looking for silver Eisenhower dollars. Becky shook her head in wonder. An American history lesson might have helped point out the obvious one-hundred-year error in their plan.

Even more bizarre was the change in Mr. Edwards. Since Tilly's hospital episode he'd become Becky's sudden ally, bending over backwards for what she might need. The shift made her leery. It simply didn't make sense. He might be buttering her up for the big slam when he ousted her as director.

When the groundbreaking ceremony was over she'd need to make some hard and concrete decisions. She fingered the letter in her dress pocket and gave it a nervous tap. The correspondence had been delivered yesterday, but she'd only retrieved the mail before leaving early this morning—hardly enough time to think through the ramifications of its contents.

Larry's red truck pulled into the parking lot, and she stepped out from the tent.

"Looks like you have everything ready," he greeted her with a smile, climbing down from the truck. "It looks great!" He slipped around to the rear of the truck and pulled back the canvas tarp. "Want to give me a hand with these chairs?"

"Sure!"

Quickly they set the folding chairs in order.

"Doing okay?" he asked with a playful smile when they met in the middle. "I don't want to wear you out before the ceremony."

Becky watched the edges of his eyes crinkle in amusement, and her heart warmed. "I'm fine," she replied. She'd miss him most of all. Given half a chance, she could easily come to love him. The thought nearly caused her spirit to collapse, and she turned away. Silently she set about finishing the chairs.

Several other church members began to arrive, and the time passed rapidly. When a substantial crowd gathered, Larry edged beside her.

"Ten more minutes," he assured her. "Then you can relax."

She looked over the crowd. "At least my parents didn't show up this morning to cause a ruckus." Then she smiled. "Maybe the Johnson boys will come forward with their posthole digger to help."

"They've already done the honors too many times." He laughed, his smile turning toward her.

She smiled back. Their "engagement" last night had been wonderful—dinner, music, and a walk along the shoreline. She'd cherish the memory forever.

"Yoo-hoo," called a woman's voice.

Becky suddenly spotted Tilly and Mr. Edwards coming toward them.

"Don't go breakin' a leg, you hear," Tilly advised with a laugh.

Mr. Edwards pumped Larry's hand with fervor. "Beautiful morning for the ceremony, don't you think?" He winked at Becky, and she blinked in surprise. "Give it a good shovelful."

Becky shook her head. "I'm not shoveling," she clarified, pointing to the canopy tent. "I'm in charge of the food."

"Nonsense," he growled, and her eyes widened. "All committee members get a dig in."

"Stop teasin' the girl," admonished Tilly. She patted Becky's arm. "You'll do just fine."

When Larry announced it was eleven o'clock, everyone gathered together. Becky tried to slink back out of the way, but Larry had a sure grip on her arm that kept her right next to him as he stepped to the makeshift microphone.

"I'm glad so many of you were able to come this morning and share with us the extraordinary gift God has given in the groundbreaking of the Thunder Bay Christian Camp." Larry stopped when the audience applauded. "By the generous donation of Kelly Enterprises we will be able to make a difference in the lives of children who visit Thunder Bay. We will have a hand in preparing our next generation." More applause erupted.

"I would like to thank the many people who made this possible." Larry rattled off several names including Becky's. After a few minutes he gave shiny new shovels to Jason, Becky, Lottie, Mrs. Phillips, and Mr. Edwards. He turned to the older man. "I'd like you to do the honor of beginning the groundbreaking."

Becky watched as Mr. Edwards's round eyes grew bigger behind his thick glasses. Larry gave him a searching glance and a nod. Something passed between them, but Becky was at a loss to explain what it was.

In less than ten minutes, the ceremony was over and the crowd descended upon the tent. Colored balloons were pumped with helium and plates filled as the happy crowd mingled until an hour passed and people moved on their way to the opening parade of the May Day celebration.

Larry came to help put away the last of the leftovers.

"We'll finish this up and head over for the festivities," Larry announced, closing the lid on the cooler. "It's time to relax."

Becky gave a weak smile and glanced about to be sure they were alone. "I wanted to wait until the ceremony was over to show you this." Quietly she pulled the folded envelope out of her pocket and extracted the letter. She handed it to Larry. "I'm afraid I'll have to move on."

Larry drew his blond brows together and looked over the letter. "Your missionary board wants you to choose another mission field?"

She nodded. "The Congo won't be open for at least one, if not two, years. They're asking all the missionaries affected to meet next week at their headquarters and discuss other possible areas." Becky gave a smile. "The good news is that the women I worked with are doing well."

"What are you planning to do?"

"To start over again, I guess."

He folded the letter and deposited it in his own pocket. She was about to protest when he held up his finger. "Are you willing to consider a full-time, paid position as camp director of Thunder Bay?"

"That's not going to happen, Larry," she replied, giving him a pointed look.

"Why?"

"There was opposition enough when I came on board without pay."

He leaned close. "Remember when we first met? You told me all I needed to have was a little bit of faith and a dream." He leaned his blond head her way. "Where's that woman today?"

"She grew up and learned to face reality."

"What if I told you the camp committee has already approved your paid position and the money has been secured?"

Becky shook her head. "I'd say you were crazy!"

"Crazy like this—" He lifted his hand and cupped her face. When he bent his head toward her she knew she was about to be kissed.

"Larry—" Her words were muffled when his lips descended on her own.

Becky couldn't think. Instead she pulled him closer until she thought she might break. Larry Newkirk was giving her a royal, truly genuine kiss, and she wasn't going to waste it— even if it might not last.

Suddenly he pulled her away and gently brushed back her hair and looked into her eyes. "Still think you're too grown up for dreams anymore?"

Wide-eyed she shook her head. "Not if the dreams are like this."

"Think this concrete-thinking man and this dreamer woman could make it as a couple if they tried hard enough?" He stroked her face with his finger. "Are you willing to give us a chance at least to see if we can make it? I know you face a bad family situation that will probably rear its head again. I can help you with that." His eyes caressed her face. "God has provided the camp director job. All you have to do is take it and let life live itself."

"And you want to do that together?" Becky raised her eyebrows in question.

"Is there something wrong with that?"

"Even after you met my family?"

"Yes!"

"Even after scaring you to death that night in the field?"

"So?"

"Even though I dream outside of the reality box?"

"Why not?" He chuckled. "Dreaming's good, isn't it?"

"I think I'm dreaming now!"

"Good!" His lips came down on hers again. "See?"

"I'm beginning to see." She suddenly kissed him with all her heart.

He pulled her back with a laugh. "I think we're making a scene." He nodded to the couple standing several yards away.

"Tilly and Van?" She laughed. "They're smiling like oversized toads!"

"Let them find their own romance," he pronounced, pulling her close again. "I've got my hands full enough."

"That's a good thing?" she questioned with a sparkle in her eyes.

"A very good thing!" With that he planted another kiss on her lips.

epilogue

Becky glanced down at the delicate folds of her simple but layered wedding dress and smiled. The serene fall island breeze caught the tips of the wispy hem encompassing her feet, and she felt its soothing motion. Larry squeezed her hand, and she lifted her face to see his warm eyes and endearing lopsided smile. Certainly the handsome, tuxedoed groom was as nervous as she. But all was right with the world today.

The newly built open-air chapel of the Thunder Bay Christian Camp still smelled of just-cut timbers and sawdust. Side by side, Becky had helped Larry and countless others construct this very first building. What better place to have the most perfect wedding to the most perfect man?

Pastor Taylor cleared his throat and Becky reluctantly drew her attention back to the ceremony. Her hand trembled as she repeated the vows and placed the wedding band onto his finger. She could hardly stand the wait as Larry did the same.

Pastor Taylor seemed to sense her impatience and gave a low chuckle. "You may now kiss the bride," he told Larry.

"With pleasure," she heard Larry murmur.

Cheers erupted from those gathered in the chapel, but Becky soon tuned out the clamor as Larry bent down ever so tenderly and gave her the kiss she'd waited for. Unbidden, a giggle escaped, and he withdrew slightly with a puzzled smile.

"What's so funny, Mrs. Newkirk?" Larry whispered into her ear.

Becky couldn't keep from grinning. "I was thinking about the first time I saw you at my door in uniform and how I thought Tilly had sent the police. Turns out, she knew more than either of us about matchmaking."

"I can't argue with her results." He laughed. "I'm sure Tilly's in her glory today over her successful venture."

"Very successful, indeed," Becky agreed.

"And you haven't seen anything yet," he teased.

"Promise?"

"Promise!" Much to her pleasure, he sealed that very promise with another kiss.

A Letter To Our Readers

Dear Reader:

In order that we might better contribute to your reading enjoyment, we would appreciate your taking a few minutes to respond to the following questions. We welcome your comments and read each form and letter we receive. When completed, please return to the following:

Fiction Editor
Heartsong Presents
PO Box 719
Uhrichsville, Ohio 44683

1. Did you enjoy reading *Thunder Bay* by Beth Loughner?
   ❑ Very much! I would like to see more books by this author!
   ❑ Moderately. I would have enjoyed it more if

   _____

   _____

   _____

2. Are you a member of **Heartsong Presents**? ❑ Yes ❑ No
   If no, where did you purchase this book? _____

   _____

3. How would you rate, on a scale from 1 (poor) to 5 (superior), the cover design? _____

4. On a scale from 1 (poor) to 10 (superior), please rate the following elements.

   ____ Heroine   ____ Plot
   ____ Hero   ____ Inspirational theme
   ____ Setting   ____ Secondary characters

5. These characters were special because? _____

_____

_____

6. How has this book inspired your life? _____

_____

_____

7. What settings would you like to see covered in future
   Heartsong Presents books? _____

_____

_____

8. What are some inspirational themes you would like to see
   treated in future books? _____

_____

_____

9. Would you be interested in reading other **Heartsong
   Presents** titles?   ❑ Yes   ❑ No

10. Please check your age range:
        ❑ Under 18   ❑ 18-24
        ❑ 25-34   ❑ 35-45
        ❑ 46-55   ❑ Over 55

Name _____

Occupation _____

Address _____

City, State, Zip_____

fresh-brewed love

4 stories in 1

*f*our women find grounds for love in these well-blended novellas. JJ is determined to make a success of her business no matter what. Kasey is the hapless victim of a matchmaking scheme. Kae fears her remaining days will be spent under the shadow of an old friendship. Carrie's desire to cover the story of a lifetime may overshadow any chances of future happiness. Can these women make the right decisions when it comes to love?

Contemporary, paperback, 352 pages, 5³/₁₆" x 8"

Heart♥ng

Presents

Great Inspirational Romance at a Great Price!

HEARTSONG
PRESENTS

If you love Christian romance...

$10.99

You'll love Heartsong Presents' inspiring and faith-filled romances by today's very best Christian authors...DiAnn Mills, Wanda E. Brunstetter, and Yvonne Lehman, to mention a few!

When you join Heartsong Presents, you'll enjoy four brand-new, mass market, 176-page books—two contemporary and two historical—that will build you up in your faith when you discover God's role in every relationship you read about!

Mass Market 176 Pages

Imagine...four new romances every four weeks—with men and women like you who long to meet the one God has chosen as the love of their lives...all for the low price of $10.99 postpaid.

To join, simply visit www.heartsong presents.com or complete the coupon below and mail it to the address provided.

- -

YES! Sign me up for Heartsong!

NEW MEMBERSHIPS WILL BE SHIPPED IMMEDIATELY!
Send no money now. We'll bill you only $10.99 postpaid with your first shipment of four books. Or for faster action, call 1-740-922-7280.

NAME _____

ADDRESS _____

CITY _____ STATE _____ ZIP _____

MAIL TO: HEARTSONG PRESENTS, P.O. Box 721, Uhrichsville, Ohio 44683
or sign up at WWW.HEARTSONGPRESENTS.COM